WHO INVITED the UNDERTAKER?

WHO INVITED the UNDERTAKER?

IVY RUCKMAN

A TRUMPET CLUB SPECIAL EDITION

Published by The Trumpet Club
666 Fifth Avenue, New York, New York 10103

Copyright © 1989 by Ivy Ruckman

ISBN: 0-440-84554-8

This edition published by arrangement with HarperCollins
Children's Books, a division of HarperCollins Publishers
Typography by Joyce Hopkins
Printed in the United States of America
October 1991

10 9 8 7 6 5 4 3 2 1
OPM

For Priscilla Sheets

WHO INVITED the UNDERTAKER?

chapter 1

The school bus had just started up Peruvian Drive.

"So when are you going to read that note?" asked Jeff.

"It says 'PRIVATE.' I'll read it when I'm private," Dale answered.

"Shoot!" Jeff slouched down in his Levi's jacket, knees against the seat in front of him. "You get a note from a girl first period and you wait all day to read it. You're big-time weird, you know that?"

Dale grinned. "Yeah, you keep telling me."

Undersized, feisty Jeff, who strained to see the world through a mop of wild hair, often saw *weird.*

3

No matter. Best friends could say exactly what they thought to each other.

For the umpteenth time, Dale pulled the folded note out of his math book where someone had stuck it that morning. He passed it under Jeff's nose, then sniffed it himself. Not a hint of perfume. He turned it over to see his name, Dale Purcell, and the word *private* printed in caps and underlined.

"How private you got to get?" Jeff asked, his eyes turning to slits. He hated being left out.

Teasingly, Dale opened the first fold.

Jeff sat up straight.

With fingertip delicacy, Dale lifted the next and the next, each crinkle of pink paper an exciting little explosion.

One more fold. By then, their heads were together, their shoulders hunched. Dale smoothed the paper over his math book. It was blank! He flipped it to the other side. Nothing there, either. What kind of stupid joke was this?

They stared at each other two whole seconds before Jeff doubled over with yuks you could hear all over the bus. Dale had a giant urge to shove him off the seat, but instead he crumpled the paper and rolled it into a ball between his palms. His first note from a girl and it didn't say anything!

Needing to cover his disappointment, Dale stuffed the wad of paper in his mouth and chewed it to a disgusting pulp. Girls could be mean as snakes when they wanted to be!

"You don't even know who sent it," Jeff said, once he quit laughing. "Who says it was a girl?"

"Yeah, but pink?"

"Ever heard of camouflage?"

Suddenly Dale was laughing, too. The idea of camouflage was pretty funny. In fact, a blank note you'd anticipated reading all day was in itself a very funny joke. Of course, he'd have preferred having Jeff's name on it instead of his.

Slick and easy, Dale slipped the spitball into Jeff's side pocket as soon as he wasn't looking. To heck with it! He had better things to think about.

"It means someone likes you is what it means," Jeff said wisely.

"Yeah? Tell me about it." Dale wasn't exactly the Tom Selleck of seventh grade. He knew that, but he wouldn't mind having someone like Lizette send him a note. One word from her would brighten any guy's life.

At his corner, Jeff jumped up and lurched away to the door, shouting "Later!" over his shoulder.

Another half mile and Dale swung off the school bus himself.

There are definitely things to be said about coming home to an empty house, he thought, unlocking the front door at 9422 Peruvian. In the old days . . . well, things had changed. He had to get used to it. Today he was glad to be alone and proud to be his own boss at twelve-going-on-thirteen.

Dale bounded up the steps to his room, tossed his books, landed with a happy squawk on his bed. Maybe Jeff was right. Maybe somebody liked him, but didn't know how to express it. Mrs. Okimoto, in first-period English, was always telling them how hard it is to put your feelings into words.

Stretched out on the bed for his first serious leisure of the day, Dale reached for a comic, then stripped back the wrapper of the Snickers bar Jeff had bought him.

One bite into the caramel-nut center, he heard the "whoosh" of the front door opening and closing downstairs. He lifted his head. Lindsey? But she had gymnastics. His little brother, Matt, didn't get home until later, either.

"Who is it?" he called.

Dale held his breath. The house was too silent if someone was down there.

His answer was a high-pitched shriek that split the air and jerked him to his feet.

Dale flung the comic, hit every third step going downstairs, the hairs on his head like wires.

It *was* Lindsey, his ten-year-old sister, standing in the kitchen pointing a stiff arm to the stove. "She did it again! She'll burn the house down!"

"Is that all?" Dale yelled. "You're screamin' your head off over that?"

He walked to the stove and switched the glowing electric burner from "8" to "Off."

"Dale! Don't you care?" Tears blobbed up in her eyes. "This is the second time."

"She's got stuff on her mind," he mumbled, his heart still beating so hard his shirt shook.

"But *twice*?"

"Don't get yourself into a lather." They were words his dad would have used. "Let's see what's to eat."

Opening the fridge, he let Lindsey squeeze past his legs for an apple.

"Are you telling her this time?" she asked. "If you don't, I'm calling Grandma long distance."

"You stupid stool pigeon, why would you do that?"

"Well, *are* you?"

"Are I what? What happened to the milk? We had a new bottle yesterday."

"Are you going to tell Mom she keeps leaving the stove on?"

"I'll tell her. Quit bugging me." There wasn't a drop of milk. That meant there wouldn't be any for breakfast, either.

When Lindsey's chin went up, he knew she wasn't through. "Grandma said I should call if anything came up I couldn't handle."

Dale spun around and treated his sister to a skin burn on the arm, the only thing he could get away with.

"You'll get it if I bruise!" she yelped.

Sometimes, like now, after she'd scared him to death, he wanted to smack her, but he didn't dare. Lindsey, the gymnast, was their family's great hope. Three hundred dollars a month's worth of Olympic potential was what she was. That's what her training cost. He himself had become the horse trader of Grant Intermediate because he never had money to spend.

"How come you're not at the gym?" he asked, getting an apple after noticing how good hers smelled.

"Wish I was! There's a meet, so Jared canceled. But I have to do warm-ups, anyway. *If* it's any of your business—" She hitched up onto a stool at the counter and took another bite. "I hate it when you're mean. What's a stool pigeon? Did you make that up?"

"Yeah, because you're always perched on a stool. You're such a shrimp you have to sit on a stool to see over the counter."

She stuck out her tongue.

"No, dummy, a stool pigeon's someone who narcs on a friend"—he gave her a sneer—"or a mother."

When the phone rang, Lindsey's superior moves paid off and she grabbed it ahead of him. Just as well. Calls from Jeff were okay, but he didn't like the calls that still came sometimes for his dad—after two years and five months.

"May I speak to Mr. Purcell, please?" some guy would say, or worse, "Call your dad to the phone, would you?"

It hadn't happened for a while, but how do you explain—when your heart comes up and stops your mouth—that a person has died and doesn't live here anymore? Once he just hung up and ran down to Jeff's.

Dale rinsed his apple at the sink. Maybe now, with Lindsey on the phone, he'd try to figure out who might have stuck that "note" in his book.

"No, I'm not supposed to tell people when . . . wait . . ." Lindsey motioned to Dale. "Maybe you should talk to my brother."

He was around the counter in nothing flat.

"Hello, this is Dale Purcell."

"Prudential Mortgage and Loan," came the voice at the other end. "Are you old enough to give your mother a message?"

"I'm old enough."

"We haven't received a mortgage payment since September first," the woman said.

Dale swallowed. So it was going to be *that* kind of call.

She went on, mentioning penalties and stuff he didn't know anything about. He nodded and went "uh-huh."

"Sorry," he said when he got a chance, "she probably just forgot."

His armpits turned prickly, the way they did at school sometimes.

Suddenly it was all too much—the stupid note, Lindsey pressed against his side trying to listen, her apple breath in his face, the embarrassment for his mom. He jabbed his sister with his elbow to move her away.

"You'll remember to tell her?" the woman said for the hundredth time.

"I won't forget!" he shouted.

And then it was over.

"I hate that lady," he said as he smacked down the receiver.

"Me, too," Lindsey added. "Anybody can forget. I forget all the time. You answer if it rings again, I'm not."

Dale walked back around the counter, frowning at the brown spot on his apple. He bit it out and spit the bad part into the sink.

Suddenly he felt a great need to be out of there and doing something. Anything! "Watch for Matt. I'm going to the store after milk if Mom has a dollar in the change box. Go see, would you?"

Lindsey didn't move at first. She just stared off, her eyes big and blue and scared. When she set her apple down on the counter, he knew the call had ruined her appetite, too.

"Something's really wrong," she said in a whisper, as if their mother could hear. "She never used to do stuff like this."

chapter 2

The shopping center and Smith's Co-op Grocery were a mile downhill from the Purcell's. Great fun getting there on a bike; misery coming back. But if his mom could walk four blocks up from the bus stop, Dale figured he could make the round trip on his old BMX.

A hero was what he'd had to become during the last two and a half years: a boy doing heroic, man-sized deeds. Of course, he was the only one who knew it.

Dale left the house with a dollar and his pack, aware as always that his legs were ridiculously long for twenty-inch wheels. But if you can't pay the mortgage, you make do on all the rest.

He waved at Lindsey standing at the door in her flowered tights, then pumped out of the driveway. Coasting downhill, the wind in his face, he all of a sudden started laughing. He was thinking about the words his mom made up to Willie Nelson's "On the Road Again." "Making do again!" she'd sing when they got in a bind. It had become the number-one hit tune at their house.

After her boyfriend, Richard, had told her her voice was as true and clear as Emmylou Harris's, she had sung all the time. Dale had loved having her sing around the house again. When Richard had quit coming, she'd quit singing, and *that* worried him more than the red-hot burners.

Five minutes later, Dale was maneuvering his beat-up bike into the rack at Smith's.

The best part of going for groceries was talking to Jeff's dad in the produce department. But he'd wait for that. First he'd check out the videos to see if any new horror films had come in. He'd also look over the Disneys for Lindsey and Matt. A person could easily spend an hour browsing.

Later, cruising up the aisle toward the milk, he remembered he was supposed to get the cheapest 2% milk and avoid the gross, fatty kind. He next headed for the produce, thinking how much money they'd save if he'd just quit drinking milk. He was old enough. Big enough, too. He'd been taller than anyone in his class since fourth grade.

He glanced up at himself in the corner shoplifting mirror that made him look squatty and bulgy-faced. He was glad he didn't look like *that*.

"Hi, Mr. Ellis," Dale said, coming up behind Jeff's dad.

"Dale, m'boy! Doin' the shoppin', are ye?" Mr. Ellis was always good for an accent.

"This much." Dale held up the carton with two fingers.

"Where's Jeff?"

"Home, I guess." Home during the school year was with his mom, Meredith Ellis—Meredith the Mortician, as Dale called her privately. Next summer when his mother had to intern, Jeff was scheduled to live with his dad.

Mr. Ellis poured mushrooms into a bin, spread them around. "Did you get an invitation to the big Wednesday-night opening?"

"What do you mean?"

"The lady out front. Didn't she grab you?"

Dale tossed an onion overhead, caught it again. "Who'd grab me?"

"Better tell your mom. The manager's starting a Single Shoppers' Event here every Wednesday—ten to midnight. That cute cookie out front is the one who talked him into it. Figure I'll put in some over-time on Wednesdays."

"Yeah, good idea."

Mr. Ellis chuckled as he swung his cart around and headed off.

"Need any help this week?" Dale called after him, thinking he could check out *Invasion of the Body Snatchers* if Jeff would go halves with him. Sometimes Jeff and he could make a couple bucks pulling off lettuce leaves or tying beets.

"Could use you guys Saturday early. Before seven, okay?" Mr. Ellis bumped rearfirst into the double swinging doors. "Better sign up to support the singles." He winked. "You could pass for eighteen easy."

Dale moved on. Yeah, sure. A twelve-year-old who doesn't shave passing for eighteen. Right, Mr. Ellis!

Out front Dale hung around a minute, thinking Cookie would offer him one of her yellow announcements, but she never did.

He slid the milk carton into his pack, yanked his bike out of the rack. Who'd want a date with her? She was about as friendly as an artichoke.

As soon as he was alone, pumping up the boulevard to Peruvian Drive, he began thinking about that glowing burner and some of the other things his mother had been doing. Or more accurately, *not* doing. He knew what was wrong. She wasn't happy. In fact, he suspected she was right back where she'd been after his dad died, and that was bad. Maybe she'd have been better off if she'd never met Richard.

Of course he wouldn't have said so last summer. Heck no, not with all the fun they were having in Richard's boat. His stomach fluttered remembering how it felt water-skiing over a syrupy-smooth lake, jumping the wake, carving designs, drifting back. He didn't know why they broke up, but it was definitely a bummer.

At the corner where Peruvian took off uphill from the boulevard, Dale stopped to catch his breath. His mom's bus would be along any minute. Maybe he'd just wait and walk up the hill with her.

He dropped his BMX on somebody's grass and found himself a spot on the curb near where the bus stopped. The cold of the concrete came right through his Levi's, but he didn't care. It would be fun to surprise her.

As usual, she was the only passenger to get off at that corner.

The doors wheezed shut, but she waited until the driver pulled away before starting up the street.

Dale grinned with suspense, then treated her to a low, slow whistle. "Hey, good lookin', what's cookin'?"

16

She swung around, her angry look vanishing instantly when she saw him. "My very own rotten kid!" She laughed. "What are you doing here?"

He picked up his bike and wheeled it toward her. "I thought you'd like some company. I've been down to Smith's for milk."

"Got a hug?" she asked as he came alongside.

He threw an uneasy look over his shoulder.

"Rather go behind a tree?" She gave him a quick squeeze, then held up a plastic tote that said *A Woman's Place Is in the Mall.* "At least we've got the fundamentals. French bread and milk. I hope you put the meat loaf in the oven."

Dale hit himself on the forehead. "I didn't, I forgot. What a pea brain!"

"Oh Dale, I've been smelling it all the way home." She sighed. "Well, dinner will just have to be late."

How could he have forgotten to put in the meat loaf?

"Sorry," he said feebly, "but I think I take after you."

"Okay, Bud, what am I getting credit for this time?"

"You forgot something today, too, but I hate to tell you."

"Tell me anyway."

"I know you didn't mean to—"

"Dale, don't always be protecting me. I'm the mom, remember? You're the kid. You can tell me anything you need to."

"Well, Lindsey was the one who found it . . ."

"Okay, hold it!" His mother grabbed his handlebars and stopped him.

"You left the back burner on," he said.

Her forehead bunched up. "I did?"

He shrugged, making like it was nothing. "I thought you'd want to know."

She kept her eyes straight ahead, but he could see a red spot coming in her cheek and knew how badly she felt. "So we're both forgetters, only I'm about ten times more dangerous than you are."

They hurried on without talking, but Dale was squeezing his brain in an effort to change the subject.

"Hey, guess what," he said when he remembered. "They're having a Singles' Night. Every Wednesday down at Smith's. Mr. Ellis said to tell you because he knew you'd be interested."

"Interested, my foot! Did Bob say that?"

"Yeah. You know . . . you're not married anymore or anything."

"Thanks for the reminder."

"Moooooom! You know what I mean." She didn't look a bit happy. "I figured you and Meredith—"

18

"Dale, please. *She* might want to shop with the single men. I don't care if I never meet anyone . . . again." She made a wipe-out gesture that looked ultrafinal to him.

"I guess you really hate Richard now, huh?"

"No, I don't hate him."

"How come you guys broke up?"

She took hold of Dale's arm and pulled him in next to her. "Never mind. What happened was that we decided—together—that our relationship wasn't going anywhere."

He liked having his mother talk to him like an adult and found himself slowing to match her pace.

"What I mean is, we weren't right for each other. He didn't have the slightest idea of what the word *commitment* meant. I miss him, I have to admit. And I've been kind of ditsy lately, as Meredith so kindly pointed out to me just yesterday. But I'm okay, and I don't want you kids to worry about whether or not I'll turn off the stove." She shook her head. "I can't believe I did that."

"We sure had fun on Richard's ski boat."

"You're right, we did."

"Did Dad know what commitment meant?"

She sucked in her breath. "Yes."

"There's something else I need to tell you," he said, remembering. "This lady on the phone, she gave me a message for you." Dale felt his mother's grip tightening on his arm. "Honestly, I hated her."

"What'd she want?"

"You have to send the house payment in right away."

When his mom's glance went all the way to the top of their oak—stripped bare for winter coming on—and he heard the "ohhh" she made, he felt terrible.

"I guess we don't have it, do we?"

"We have it. I'm in arrears, I know. I'll have to dip into the insurance and pay the penalty, that's all."

She waited for Dale to put his bike away, then they walked toward the house with their arms around each other.

"Bill collectors can't eat us," she reminded him. "They can only buzz around and annoy us."

When she started singing "We'll get by—" he decided she was a very brave mom. He also decided she needed help whether she knew it or not. Three kids, a house, an old Ford, and Lindsey with her stupid Olympic potential. Talk about problems! Getting a non-note from some nonentity at school was nothing compared with what his mom faced every day.

Maybe *she* didn't want to meet anybody, but he figured there must be some grown men in this world who had commitment and a good job both. If she was too busy to look around . . . well . . . he wasn't.

"Mooooom," Lindsey called from the rec room as soon as they walked in, "come see the mark Dale left on my arm."

His mother was just turning an evil eye on him when his red-cheeked brother, Matt, burst in the front door swinging his lunch pail.

"Guess what!" Matt announced like Dan Rather winding up for the news. "I threw up today, but the nurse gave me some pink stuff and now I'm good as new." He wriggled out of his jacket, leaving it where it fell. "She said I should stay home tomorrow if I'm still doing it."

Six-year-olds! Dale shuddered. Maybe Richard had his reasons.

chapter 3

The next Friday at school Dale walked into first-period English to find four people in line at the pencil sharpener. Essay day, he remembered with a jolt.

"Hey, give me some paper," he said, grabbing Jeff before they split up for their desks. "I'll pay you back."

With exaggerated patience, Jeff set down his books and ripped two sheets out of his notebook.

"You wouldn't make it through seventh grade without me, Purcell. When do I get it back? You've used up half my spiral."

"Look, I got a new comic at home. It's yours. Honest."

"Big deal!" Jeff muttered.

"Thanks." Dale moved on to join the other back-row bunglers. He often wondered why they didn't just put up a sign: *These puny little desks in the back reserved for giants, snorers, druggies, and other unsavory types the teacher doesn't want under her nose.* Sometimes being tall was the pits.

He pulled a pencil out of his rear pocket before sitting down, at the same time wondering what subject Mrs. Okimoto would give them to write about today. Their first assignment of the year had been an account of how it felt to be drowning. All of it made up.

She'd looked horrified when the kids protested. "Don't you have imaginations?" she'd asked. "Oh, sorry, you never use them, how would you know?"

The next week's assignment was to write up the tongue-lashing Benjamin Franklin might have given his oldest son when he forgot to feed the chickens. For that one she'd insisted on research. He'd ended up knowing old Ben intimately. So had his mom, who'd helped.

Later on, they'd had to hand in two pages describing the Denver Broncos' locker room before a Super Bowl game. "In ink and double-spaced or forget it," was what she'd said. He'd gotten an A on that one.

Students either loved her or hated her. At least Fridays in her class were never dull, and she was interesting to look at. Her mascara always matched her necklace or her blouse.

A hush fell over the room as soon as the bell rang—astonishing in itself for intermediate school.

"Today we're going to write about families," Mrs. Okimoto said with the special smile she dispensed with writing assignments.

Dale looked at his neighbor, who looked back with the same zonked expression he wore every day. The subject of families apparently didn't interest him, either.

"Jennifer," the teacher began, "define the word *family* for us."

Jennifer sat front and center and could define anything.

"A family would be a group of people," she began in her crisp way of speaking. "Parents, children. And they live together." She stopped to think.

"They don't have to live together," Carol jumped in. "I mean, my grandparents are part of my family and they don't live with us."

"You can be a family without kids," came another voice.

"So . . . what else, what else?" the teacher said,

her hands going like a choir director's pulling out notes.

Others jumped in until *family* got to be a very large word, including even their school family of 537 students with the principal at its head.

Then Mrs. Okimoto stepped to the board, motioning for order. "We've been speaking very generally, but now I want to narrow our subject to one family—yours. No one else's. Your particular family. It's different from anyone else's in the world. And your role in that family is unique."

Dale looked around. They were a melting pot all right, with Vietnamese, blacks, whites, and a straight-A kid who spoke Spanish as well as English. Mrs. Okimoto herself was Japanese-American.

"Let's brainstorm first. Start with what family members do for each other." She picked up the chalk.

Words like *love, listen, support, respect* flew to the front of the room.

"Now what do families do together?"

Play, fight, talk, eat, clean house, spend money, grow up.

Dale heard someone, down low, say "Make love." Guys snickered, but the unflappable Okimoto just kept writing.

"Worry," Dale added when he got a chance, thinking his family had been doing more than its share lately.

Finally she wrote a sentence on the board: "The thing about my family is—" and said she was more interested in what made each family different as a group than in what made them alike. She also reminded them that families and living patterns sometimes changed, that they shouldn't feel weird or anything if their group wasn't traditional.

"In 1960 only one child in ten was living in a single-parent household," she explained. "By 1986 that figure had risen to twenty-four percent. That's almost one fourth. I'm a single parent myself, so I know a little about it."

It was nice of her to tell them that, Dale thought. He'd never have guessed. They all knew she had a son because he was a seventh grader at their school, but not having a husband came as a surprise. Funny how you always thought of the word *parent* as two. In fact, leaving off the *s*, it looked to him as if you'd forgotten something.

A minute later, Mrs. Okimoto got them into what she called "buzz boxes"—four desks facing—so they could talk a little before writing. Lizette usually joined his group, along with yakky Carol and the sleeping giant on his left.

"My family's so ordinary we're boring," Carol complained over the scraping noises of desks being moved. "Think I'll make something up."

Lizette tossed her gorgeous hair. "Me too. I'm the only one left at home, so we're really boring." She asked the other kid, "How about you, Carter?"

"The usual," he said. "Mom, Dad, a brother and sister. But we all race snowmobiles. That's what I'll write about."

"No kidding?" Lizette's voice swooped up an octave. "That does make you a different family. I don't know anyone who races snowmobiles."

"Yeah." He actually looked happy for once. "My dad's a dealer."

Dale was racking his brain, trying to think what he could possibly write that would be interesting. He suspected he was the only one whose father had died, but he wasn't about to do an essay on that.

"So?" Carol swung back to look at Dale. "What about you?"

"There's my mom," he began, "and Lindsey. She's ten. And I have a little brother. Matt's in first grade and kind of goofy."

"You're a single-parent household?" Carol asked, her eyes widening.

"Yeah, I guess . . . if that's what you want to call it."

"Hey, look, this is neat—" she couldn't resist pointing out, "the figures are right. She said one out of four, didn't she? There are three normals here and one—"

"*Ab*normal?" Dale said, too loud.

"No," she giggled, "of course not. I mean, you know what I'm saying. She just quoted those figures

27

and . . . here we are. The perfect example."

Lizette rolled her eyes. "Grab a dictionary back there, Dale. I always like to look up a word. It gives me better ideas."

Dale was glad to stand up and do something. He pulled a dictionary from the bookcase behind him and flipped pages to get to the *F*'s.

He shoved it across his desk and onto Lizette's. "Here."

Her finger slid down the page. "Familiarity . . . familiarize . . . familiar spirit . . . family!" Lizette read all eight definitions while the rest of them sat and listened. All eight!

"There," she finished, popping shut the dictionary and looking at Dale with twinkly eyes. "Family comes between *familiar spirit* and *famine* if you want to look it up again at home."

When Mrs. Okimoto rapped on the board and said it was time to push back their desks and write, Lizette smiled right at him. Suddenly Dale knew why she'd taken up all their time. It was for him, and to stifle Carol, who didn't know when to shut up. It was to spare his feelings.

The next thirty minutes he never once swallowed the grin on his face. Lizette was too classy to put a blank note in someone's book, he knew that. But wouldn't it be radical if she had?

chapter 4

It was a few days later when Dale padded upstairs in his stocking feet with newspapers under both arms. If he hurried he could finish before Lindsey or Matt got home. Matt, especially, had never kept a secret in his life. He blabbed everything before you even finished telling *him*.

"Your basic motormouth" was the way Meredith Ellis described him. At least Dale had hoped she was talking about Matt, not him.

Anyway, it was good to feel in control for once. He'd put the clothes in the dryer, and the macaroni and cheese was in the oven on 325°. He'd also split four carrots and arranged them in the bottom half of a green pepper—his own idea. If he'd had black olives to stick on each carrot point, they'd have thought they were at the Hilton or something.

The night before, he'd heard his mother crying when she thought no one was around. That was enough to push a person over the edge. He hated having his mother cry. It wasn't loud crying, like Lindsey howling. She was just making soft, sad noises that no one was supposed to hear. Then she blew her nose, turned out the lights, and went on to bed.

It had taken him forever to get to sleep. He couldn't stand it that his mother was unhappy again.

Going through each of the newspapers now, he pulled the business section, then cut out the columns he wanted, arranging them by dates on the bed. The leftovers he piled on the floor. He'd just got a good start with a black Magic Marker when the doorbell rang.

It was Jeff, standing there on the front porch with his hand out.

"The comic you owe me," he said. No "Hi" or "Whatcha doing?" or anything, just "Gimme the comic." He'd make a great bill collector, Dale thought.

"They don't live here," Dale said, slamming the door in Jeff's face.

"Yeah?"

Dale opened up again. "If you're selling something—"

Jeff pushed his way in and they scuffled around until Dale pinned him against the wall and banged his head a couple of times.

"Why do I come over here?" Jeff moaned. "I always get injured."

"So who asked you to come? I'm busy, anyway." He opened the door again, inviting him to leave, but it only gave Jeff a chance to go bounding up the stairs instead. Dale was right behind him.

"Don't go in there!" he yelled. "I mean it, Jeff, I'll kill you!"

Dale heard a big crashing sound: Jeff, slipping on the pile of newspapers. When he got there himself, his friend was wide-eyed and on the floor.

"Booby-trap the place, why don'tcha?" Jeff said, sitting up and working his shoulders back into his Levi's jacket.

Dale grabbed him by the sleeve and pulled him up, laughing like crazy. "How come you never listen to me?"

Now what? Dale thought, knowing it was too late to hide anything. Not only had Jeff seen the clippings, he already had one in his hand. He scanned it, looked up. "What are you doing, anyway?"

Dale just scratched his head. He knew he could

trust Jeff, but what would he think? He ended up hesitating so long Jeff drew his own conclusions.

"You going to call 555-DATE? I did that once."

"Heck, no," he said as he gathered the extra papers off the floor and threw them outside in the hall. "I'm checking to see what people are advertising for. You know, you can find some hot deals on stuff in the ads."

"Yeah?"

Jeff didn't believe him for a second, but Dale went on.

"Look at this one. 'Stun gun. Personal protection. Closeout. Best price yet.' " He stuck it under Jeff's nose. "How'd you like to have one of those? When old Mark Letterman corners you after school, you just whip out your stun gun and let him have it in the face. Oh, man, that'd be so cool!"

Jeff shouldered a gun, took aim. "Yak-a-tak-a-tak-a-tak-a-tak-tak!" He staggered backward into Dale's dresser, forcing the top drawer shut.

"It's not a machine gun, dummy! A stun gun's a little bitty thing. I bet it would fit in your pocket."

"Okay, Purcell!" Jeff had stopped playing dumb. "Tell me the truth."

Normally he'd bust Jeff a good one for calling his bluff, but he decided to let it slide. Switching into cool-and-knowledgeable, he simply leaned over the bed and stacked his clippings. "I'm making a study," he said. "I'm trying to figure out how people meet each other. You know, people like my mom. Singles."

"Oh." Jeff actually looked relieved. "Because Richard cut her off?"

"She says it was mutual, but I don't think she's getting over it. Like she's doing all these dumb things. You know what happens when you leave a cup of flour out of a chocolate cake you're stirring up? It turns out brownies. That's the latest. She did that Saturday."

Jeff's eyebrows went up. "That's my kind of crazy."

"Yes, but there's worse. I happen to know she went to a fortune-teller with your mom. It cost her thirty bucks. No kidding. Old Lindsey has holes in her leotards and I've got a shop fee coming up. Thirty whole bucks, Ellis!"

Dale flopped back across his bed and stared at the ceiling.

"Why don't you just tell her to shape up?"

"Ever told your mom to shape up?"

Jeff drew a finger across his throat.

"What I was doing, see, was trying to find out how people worded these 'I'd like a date' ads. There must be ten in the paper every day."

Jeff started to grin. "You're going to put one in for your mom?"

"Maybe. Got any better ideas?"

"There's that singles' night at the store. It's all my dad talks about."

"She won't go."

"Let me see some of those." Jeff grabbed the pile out of Dale's hand and started to read.

"Here's one. Hey, this is good. It's . . . you know . . . subtle."

"What do you mean, *subtill*?"

"You know, it's not embarrassing."

Dale leaned over his friend's arm as Jeff read aloud: " 'To Honda Prelude. Call me. Black Corvette. Seen you on freeway Sunday afternoon. 555-4212. Gerald.' "

They looked at each other, mouths open.

"You think Honda Prelude ever called him?" Jeff asked. "Boy, I would. Black Corvette, jeez!"

"We could call and ask him," Dale said, thinking he wouldn't dare. Not really.

Jeff backhanded him across the chest. "Sure! Call and ask if it worked. Then you wouldn't have to waste your money."

"Nah! With our car, you kidding? Get this: 'To black BMW. Call me. Fairmont Ford wagon with hubcab missing.' " Jeff fell over laughing, but Dale wasn't finished.

" 'Saw you at First Federal outdoor bank depository Saturday where I was getting a loan. Cathy.' "

Dale made like he was barfing.

Suddenly every ad they read came out funny: " 'Round Trip to LAX,' " Jeff shouted, adding, "Bet that stands for laxative."

"Free Acne Study" came out lots funnier than it should have.

They were shrieking when they came to "Pie fights unlimited. Give a party everyone will remember. Have a pie fight!" They slapped and hollered and beat on each other until Dale slid onto the floor, tears smearing his cheeks.

Things got so wild they didn't hear Lindsey when she came home from the gym. She could have spied on them and they wouldn't have known, except she had to stick her head in to see what was going on.

"What's so funny?" she asked.

Dale jumped to his feet. "Don't you ever knock? Get out of my room."

"What are you guys laughing about?"

"Listen," Jeff broke in, "here's one for you, Lindsey. Get this: 'Looking for 25 overweight people for study. Hourly pay. Call between 9:00 and 2:00, Monday through Friday.' "

Dale snorted. "Yeah, Lindsey, you could make some money throwing your weight around. That's what you're always doing anyway."

She made a face. "Verrrrrrry funny."

"Beat it!" Dale shoved her out and closed the

35

door. He turned back to Jeff, his finger flying to his lips. "Ssshhh. If she finds out, I'll end up in the compost. Come on, you got to help me. I have to word the ad right or this isn't going to work."

Turning suddenly businesslike, they spread the columns out around them on the floor, then began marking what Jeff called the "love ads."

"Most of them say how tall," Dale noticed. "I'll have to ask Mom how tall she is if we're going to do this right."

"She's average. Just say 'average looks.' That'll cover it."

"Are you kidding? You can't say *average*. Would you pick up the phone to call somebody average?"

Jeff shrugged. "If she owned a new Honda Prelude."

"Here's one. Hey, listen to this. It's perfect." Dale leaned back and read, " 'Likeable, levelheaded lady loves laughter, loyalty, little ones.' All those *L*'s—get it?—and her name's Linda. That's what we need, something clever, eye-catching. It doesn't say anything about looks . . . doesn't even mention her car."

"That means she's poor and ugly," Jeff concluded.

"You think so? Okay, so that's why we have to be careful. People are going to read between the lines."

"How do you plan to pay for this?"

"My birthday's coming up. Grandpa always sends me money. Ten, anyway."

Dale stood, got a crumpled paper out of the wastebasket and smoothed it out. "Maybe we should 'cluster,' like Mrs. Okimoto does on the board. Want to?"

"Yeah! Put down all the words that describe her, then figure out what to do with them. Good idea." Jeff concentrated a minute. "Start with *nice*. I've always thought your mom was real nice."

Dale gave him a hopeless look. "Nice! What kind of a dumb word is that?"

"What's wrong with it?"

"You know, it's one of those words you wouldn't say about yourself. You don't go around describing yourself as 'nice.' Use your head."

"You could say 'foxy,' except—"

"Except she's not. I mean, Mom's okay, but foxy is—"

"You're right, she's not a fox."

"Kind!" Dale sat up. "She's the kindest person I know. Sometimes it gets her in trouble she's so kind. But that's one of those words like 'nice,' isn't it?"

"Put it down anyway. Now—what else?" They both thought awhile.

"She's smart, isn't she?" Jeff asked.

"Not lately."

"Hard working, I bet."

Dale looked up, smiled. "You're a genius. That's what Dad used to call her, 'my hard-working wife.'" Dale laughed, remembering. "Mom hated it. Sometimes she'd throw a sofa pillow at him, then he'd grab her and they'd kiss." For a minute he was back in time, on a Sunday afternoon watching football with his dad. His mom would bring in the popcorn and her book. . . .

The memory popped. He was in his own room staring at Jeff's knees.

Soberly he wrote down "hard working."

In half an hour they were finished. They read the ad over five or six times, out loud, to see how it would sound to a perfect stranger—the committed, well-to-do, and possibly handsome stranger they had in mind, who'd be reading his paper alone on a Sunday morning . . . somewhere . . . in his penthouse apartment or on his boat.

"It's a masterpiece," Dale declared as he dug out the Power Pack comic he owed Jeff. "I think our troubles are over."

chapter 5

The day after his birthday Dale typed up the ad for the *Gazette* and put it in the mail. Amazingly, Jeff and he had kept it to the twenty-word limit plus phone number, so seven bucks covered it. One dollar at a time—most of his birthday check from Grandpa Sherwood—went into the envelope with the message.

"Once I put this in the slot," he told Jeff at the blue collection box, "it's done. There's no backing out."

Jeff shrugged. "So go ahead and do it."

Easy for you, thought Dale. It's not your mother

we're putting up for grabs. He shoved the envelope into the slot, listened for it to land. He sighed as they walked away. "Just once I'd like to have worries I could handle."

"Yeah, like what?"

"Oh, like stabilizing the number-three reactor at the nuclear plant, maybe."

They'd decided the ad should run Thursday through Sunday so it would get the most readers. With a little luck, by Saturday night Cathy Purcell would be humming "Forever and Ever, Amen" as she dressed for her first date with Blake. "Blake" was the code name Jeff and he were using. If the guy calling turned out to be Archibald or Terrance, his mom might end up saying "Thanks, but no thanks."

Dale's big problem after sending in the ad was deciding if it would be better to be home when the calls started coming Thursday or to be gone. And what about Lindsey? Could he trust her not to tell? Wednesday morning he went to school early to discuss strategy, but his partner in crime had other ideas.

Jeff met him on the steps. "Man, we lucked out today! I know where she is." *She* meaning Lizette, the girl every right-thinking guy in seventh grade adored.

Dale sighed. It didn't matter to Jeff that his mom

was on the brink of romance, or that he'd be an endangered species if things didn't work out. Once Jeff decided it was a good day to follow girls, that's what they'd do.

Cruising, of course, was not a new activity. It was something they did at least once a week. It was also something they didn't tell anyone they did. Usually they weren't particular about who they followed, but Jeff had this continuing thing about Lizette—not too different from *his* thing about Lizette. Way back in first grade, Jeff had given her the ring his dentist gave him. The next day he'd found it stuffed into an envelope and crammed inside his desk. Six years later, he was still feeling rejected.

Their usual tack was to get a lively conversation going so the girls wouldn't suspect anything. They'd walk along, laughing and making rude cracks at each other. They might stop and spray water at the cooler, or yell to some guy they knew. Sometimes Lizette or Megan or Dana would give them a dirty look over her shoulder, but mostly the girls just went sailing above the seventh-grade masses like highborn princesses.

A couple of times Dale suspected the girls themselves were out following the boys, though Jeff said they had more serious stuff on their minds. But what if the girls *were* following the boys, and the boys were following the girls, and the girls behind them were following them . . . and you yelled a big "About face!" and everyone collided?

Actually, he liked the idea of smashing into Lizette, so he usually took part in the surveillance, but this morning he was beginning to feel bummed. Who was more important, his mom or the class goddess? Whose life was at stake, anyway—Jeff's or his?

"So when was the last time you spoke to her?" Dale couldn't resist asking as they hurried toward the west hall where Jeff had spotted her.

"I don't know. A year ago, I think."

"Gol, give it up!"

"I can't! I dream about her. I think about her all through social studies because I can see her in that class. Especially when she leans forward on her elbows. Her face and her arms just barely come into view."

As it turned out, they followed Lizette and her two friends twice around the halls, until they stopped at the trophy display and wouldn't budge. At that point they had to slide by.

"All right, Ellis," Dale said, jumping at a chance to talk, "what happens if Mom waits for me to answer the phone, like she does half the time?"

"It's her arms," Jeff whispered. "Is it possible to be in love with a girl's arms?"

"Arms! Are you crazy? I'm talking about tomorrow night when the old *Gazette* comes out."

"Yeah, but listen. I want you to look at Lizette's arms sometime. I mean, really look at them. The way they kind of curve, you know? And in the sun, the fuzzy blond hairs—"

"Jeff, I'm gonna lose my breakfast if you don't shut up."

"Okay, okay, but what about *you*? I mean, I see you staring at her in Okimoto's class."

Dale burst out laughing. "I'm in love with her hair."

"See, see?" Jeff shoved him against a locker front. "Arms, hair, what's the difference? Think there's something wrong with us?"

"Heck no. Didn't you learn anything at sixth-grade maturation?"

"Yeah, but this year we got to wait all the way to spring to see those movies," Jeff grumbled. "I could be married by then."

They went on talking about girls after school at Jeff's house for a whole hour. An hour was as much time as they ever gave to studying bike catalogs or playing Nintendo. For some reason, Dale ended up feeling guilty. Girls were fascinating, particularly Lizette, but what had he learned? Nothing. And he still didn't know if it was better to be wisely absent come Thursday.

By the time he got home from Jeff's, the snow

was flying and Meredith Ellis was having coffee at the kitchen counter with his mom. The table wasn't set yet, which meant Lindsey was still at the gym.

"Hi ya, Dale," Meredith said, looking up as he walked in. "How you doing?"

She was a great one for hugging, but this time she reached out and grabbed his hand. For a second, he thought she was going to take a bite out of it. "Warm, firm, living flesh!" she cackled, kneading it between her own.

Now that she was learning how to embalm, she was always saying weird stuff like that.

Retrieving his hand, Dale headed toward the fridge. "What's new?" he asked Meredith, to be polite.

"You don't want to know," she answered glumly.

His mother thought Meredith was exotic with her Chinese-style haircut and far-out clothes, but *spooky* came closer as far as he was concerned.

His mom got up, headed for the coffee maker. "Your room?" she said, nudging him as she went past. "Vermin village, know what I mean?"

"Okay, Inspector 12!" He glanced across the counter at Jeff's mom. "I been over at your house."

"We deduced as much," she said.

"Dinner will be late tonight," his mother told him, "so you'll have time to do a good job on your room. Dust and vacuum both, okay?''

He sensed she was trying to get rid of him, but she probably needed someone to talk to as much as he did. Jeff and he had covered a lot of territory themselves since breakfast.

Cold shivered up his spine imagining how much his mom would have to talk about once the ad appeared in the *Gazette.* He also knew she might just kill him. She might feed him to the disposal, one finger at a time, so he could never write a personal ad again.

Balancing nachos on a glass of milk, Dale proceeded around the corner to the living room, where he could stretch out and still hear what they were saying. Eavesdropping was more fun than worrying any day.

He flipped on the TV and checked the channels, to make things seem normal, then turned it off and rattled the paper a second. He could hear Meredith say, ''—but before that, she said I should burn my bridges. As if I had all these bridges. I don't know, Cathy, how much can you believe? I'm just too much of a realist.''

''You—a realist?'' came his mom's voice. ''Hah!''

''Well, whatever—''

''But you said you asked Sylvia about me. What'd she say?''

Sylvia! His hunch was right! Meredith had spent

another thirty bucks seeing that card reader.

"Let me tell you first—" Meredith paused, and Dale strained to catch her words.

"You're getting off," his mom cut in. "Go back to what you asked Sylvia about me. And I want to know exactly how you phrased it."

"I said—"

"Wait." There was a five-second silence. "Dale?"

He leaped, hearing his name. "What?"

"Run out to the street and get the mail, please. It's still in the box. Right this minute, you hear?"

She didn't fool him. She didn't want him listening. He took his time tying up his shoes, but it was long enough to hear Meredith say that, according to the cards, his mother was going to have a pleasant surprise. It would come in the mail or by way of the phone, but she wouldn't have long to wait.

The phone! The words hit him like a ten-ton demolition ball. What did it mean? How could the swami know he'd sent in an ad to get his mom a date?

"Move it, Dale!" came his mother's voice, jerking him to his feet.

He was in such a hurry to get back inside, he didn't check the mail for free samples or anything, just grabbed it up and brought it in. He handed the pile to his mom, then went after his glass for a refill. He hoped he hadn't missed too much. Meredith was now talking about herself—which bridges she planned to burn and which she didn't.

He'd just taken the milk carton out of the fridge and turned around when he saw his mom pull two tickets and a piece of paper out of an envelope.

"From Richard," she said to Meredith in a shaky voice, "tickets for the Dwight Yoakam concert Saturday night."

Dale stood there paralyzed. Saturday night! That would ruin everything. But maybe the tickets were the big surprise that showed up in her cards. Oh boy, now he was believing that stuff! But if she and Richard got together again, what about "Blake," and what about his own seven bucks down the drain?

His mom and Meredith just sat there, staring at each other, Meredith with her mouth open. When his mother finally spoke, it was to snap at him.

"Upstairs, Dale! I want that room in order before dinner. Do you know what the word *eviction* means?"

He had an idea.

Just then Matt came crashing in the front door, his coat half off and dragging. "Shawn and I got in a wreck with our Big Wheels," he shouted, "and she made us stay in second recess." The coat went flying. "Then Shawn got mad and kicked me, and I cried—" He'd have the whole day's events told before he ever got to the kitchen.

Dale sighed and took off upstairs with the vacuum. He'd think about Lizette while he worked. He for sure didn't want to think about what would happen tomorrow night when the *Gazette* hit the streets.

chapter 6

The only good thing that happened at school Thursday was having Mrs. Okimoto choose his paper to read to the class. She didn't tell whose it was, but he thought Lizette knew because she kept turning around and smiling.

At first Dale had thought of skipping the essay assignment. What could he say about the Purcells that didn't begin and end with "someone's missing"? Their family was like a bike that had been stripped of its gears. You might call it a ten-speed still, but a vital part was definitely missing.

His father's death from a heart attack had meant

he'd had to grow up faster than maybe he was supposed to. Like not acting scared during a rattling thunderstorm when he was alone tending Matt. Or telling off the pervert who called up and talked sick. Or sitting with his mom in church sometimes instead of with his friends so she wouldn't be alone.

Sure, he had stuff to write about—everybody does—but he didn't know how to put any of it so he wouldn't sound like he was whining.

It wasn't until the paper was almost due that Mrs. Okimoto said something in class that got him started.

Humor, she wrote on the board.

"You can say some very serious things with humor." Then she put *anecdotes* on the board next to *humor*. "I'm hoping to find a few funny stories in your essays tomorrow."

Alone in his room that night, he'd written the whole thing in an hour, except for copying it over. "My Life as Man of the House" was his title.

It blew his mind that his was the first paper Mrs. Okimoto read aloud to the class. Thank heavens the kids laughed in the right places. He was grinning off and on himself, though his ears were going up in flames the whole time.

His first anecdote went back to when he was ten, to a time his mom was expecting an old friend who was passing through town and had called.

50

"Just be nice to Greg if he gets here while I'm gone," she'd instructed Dale as she tore off to the bakery for some goodies.

Minutes later, sure enough, the doorbell rang. Dale had promptly invited the guy in, remembering how polite his dad would have been. All along he was thinking it was his mom's friend, when the man was really some kind of door-to-door missionary. They had drunk lemonade and talked about Jesus a whole hour before his mom came home and rescued him.

The last story in his essay involved Matt. Alone one day, Matt and he had captured a shiny black spider. They'd forced it kicking and spitting into a jar, then spent the whole afternoon finding flies for it. He'd had a ton of fun, explaining to Matt, as their dad had to him, how important it was for people to take care of helpless animals. It wasn't until his mom saw Matt's crayon picture that night—of the black widow's red hourglass—that she'd gone screaming up the stairs to find their new pet.

"Her name's Charlotte," Matt had yelled at her back, "and she's gonna make a web, so don't hurt her!"

Mrs. Okimoto waited for the class to quit laughing before reading the final paragraph. "In conclusion, I've decided the man of the house ought to be a man."

When Mrs. Okimoto looked up that time, she smiled straight at him. Then she read his ending: "A growing boy ought to be a growing boy. So why don't I get my role straightened out? My mom always asks. Well, maybe I will someday. I'll never be able to fill my dad's shoes, I know that. But sometimes it feels good just to go clomping around in them."

Arriving home after school Thursday night, Dale was excited and full of regret by turns. He wanted to tell someone about his paper, but no one was there to tell. At the same time, he was so worried about the personal ad he was almost sick.

His accomplice had promised to come over after he finished his chores. "In case of fireworks," he'd said, laughing bravely because it wasn't *his* mom. So far he hadn't shown up yet.

Several times Dale walked to the phone, thinking, Where are you, old bud, now that I need you? But calling Jeff would only delay things. Besides, the phone would soon be ringing for his mom. He couldn't tie up the line.

He took hamburger out of the freezer and swept the garage like he was supposed to. He watched a little TV. Nothing helped. Sitting there on the floor, he concentrated to see if he could feel his legs growing. Sometimes he thought he could actually feel cells multiplying. It was a weird sensation, but what it really meant was that he was having the heebie-jeebies big time. Finally, all he could do was hang around the front window watching for the paperboy.

At the shrill sound of the phone, his arms and legs went flying like the *Wizard of Oz* scarecrow's.

"Hello," he squeaked into the mouthpiece a second later.

"I'm calling about your ad in the paper." A woman's voice! What was a woman doing calling his mom? "Is this the right party?" she asked.

"I don't know. What ad?"

She laughed nervously. "Well, did you put an ad in the *Gazette*?"

Dale cleared his throat and tried to deepen his voice. "Actually, yes."

"You sound awfully . . . young."

"Oh, the ad isn't for me. It's for someone else. Could I take your name and—"

Click. She hung up. For a minute Dale just stood there, staring at the phone in his hand. He listened again, but sure enough she was gone. Gol, why'd she hang up?

He took a deep breath and leaned against the wall next to the kitchen phone. If Jeff didn't come pretty soon! Maybe it would be smart to take the phone off the hook for a while.

The doorbell! He tore across the house, yelling

"Come on in, Jeff!" He yanked open the front door. "Where you been? I already had one call, but she hung up on me."

"She!" Pint-size Jeff pulled off his coat and tossed it on the banister.

"Some nutsy lady. I bet there are people who call numbers from the personals all the time, just to have someone to talk to. And guess what? She said I sounded 'young.' "

"Uh-oh."

"What do you mean, 'Uh-oh'?"

"Let me answer if it rings again. My voice is deeper than yours."

He was right. Jeff might look like a fourth grader, but he was already getting hormones. He could pass for fifteen on the phone.

They'd just got into milk and bologna sandwiches at the counter when the phone rang again.

Jeff bounced up, but he had to wash down a bite before he could talk. After the "hello" he listened for what seemed to be an awfully long time. Then he asked, "So you like boats, too? Do you water-ski?"

Dale sat there, glued to his stool. "Make him call back," he mouthed.

Jeff frowned and shook his head. "No," he went on, very adultlike, "I don't have any children. How about you?"

Whaaaaaaaat? Why was *Jeff* having the conversation? Dale grabbed a notepad and pencil, scrawled, "Have him call back! 5:30," and shoved it in front of Jeff.

"I think there's been some mistake," Jeff said finally. "Yeah, I feel the same way—but I didn't put that ad in the paper. Sure, yeah . . . well, I'm sorry, too . . . okay, then, good-bye!"

Dale was on his feet screaming. "You idiot! That might have been the one we were after. Why didn't you tell him to call back?"

"It wasn't a *him,* that's why. It was some dumb lady and she gave me an earful. She was starting to like me, I think. They must have got the ad wrong down there. I don't know what's going on!"

They faced off a minute, angry eyes boring into each other's, then Dale swung around to check the clock. "The paper's got to be here by now."

They took off, squeezing to see who could get through the door first, grabbing each other's T-shirts, then shoving for sidewalk space. Jeff spun onto the driveway first, but it was Dale who scooped up the Thursday news lying there in its clear plastic wrapper.

Back inside, they quickly found the personals column.

"Here it is!" Jeff shouted. "And they put hearts over it, like we said."

"So what's it say? How come we're getting calls from *women*? Oh man, I have a feeling—" Dale pulled the paper away from Jeff.

"Don't hog it! Come on, read it out loud."

"It goes, 'C. likes cooking, country music—' "

"How come you didn't you use her name? I thought we decided you'd use her name."

"I changed my mind. I figured . . . you know . . . to protect her privacy, in case some nut . . ."

"Yeah, yeah, all right. So start at the top again."

" 'C. likes cooking, country music, and commitment. Hard working, but hilarious. Loves boats and books both. Must see to believe!' " He swung around to face Jeff. "That's just the way we wrote it."

The phone rang again, but this time Dale grabbed it.

"Hello," came a musical voice from the other end. Another woman! What was going on?

"Hello!" Dale answered warily.

"Commitment and country music both?" she asked. "In the same person? You expect people to believe that?"

"Yes, ma'am."

"What's your name? I bet it's Charlie."

"Charlie?" He gave a nervous laugh. "No, the *C* stands for Cathy."

Big silence. Then, "Am I talking to a member of my own sex?"

"No, but—" Suddenly it dawned on him, what he'd done by not using his mom's name, and he threw the receiver back on the hook.

"Jeff, I blew it!" He covered his face with his hands and slumped down the wall to the floor. "She's gonna kill me!"

Cool Genius Jeff stepped over him, took a big wad of gum out of his mouth, rolled it into a ball, and placed it so the phone would give a busy signal to anyone trying to call. His face wore a proud expression when he said, "She won't kill you if the phone can't ring . . . now will she?"

Dale sat on the floor, staring up at his friend. "You strawhead! We're talking four whole days. Are you kidding?"

Then they heard the garage door going up and Dale knew his mom and Matt were home. They'd been out shopping for winter boots, which meant she'd be in the worst possible mood. And dinner hadn't even been started.

In a flash Dale was on his feet, scrunching up the personals page and jamming it into the wastebasket under the sink. He then hauled four plates out of the cupboard and shoved them into Jeff's stomach. "Set the table!" he ordered. "Knives and forks, too, quick!"

Into the refrigerator for salad greens, he began tearing up lettuce like a madman.

"Invite me for dinner as soon as she walks in. And make it sound normal. Oh, man, I'm dead!"

"You and me both," Jeff moaned, "but get this! If she won't let you, *I*'m outta here!"

chapter 7

By the time Dale's mother and Matt came in from the garage, the table was set and Dale was energetically whacking up radishes on the cutting board.

Matt tossed a package onto the counter.

"Guess what *I* got!" he shouted, filling the air with bubble-gum breath.

Dale rolled his eyes at Jeff. "Let's see. My guess is . . . you got a Honda Interceptor in there . . . with a 500-cc engine."

Jeff bent his ear to the package. "Good guess! I can hear it revvin'."

"Nooooooo," Matt groaned. "Come on, what'd I get?"

"How about a twenty-foot boa constrictor?"

Matt slipped the plastic off the box, lifted the lid with his teeth, stood back. "Ta daaaaa!"

"Combat boots!" Dale said. "Hey, like G.I. Joe. I'm gonna be jealous."

Matt was pleased as anything. "And look! Tractor tread on the soles."

Dale was so nervous he jumped when his mom kissed him from behind.

"Thirty-eight dollars worth of tread," she said at his ear, then, smiling at Jeff, "Where have you been lately?"

"I don't know. Hanging out, I guess. Say, could Dale eat at our house tonight?"

"Does your mom still think I'm starving him?" Mrs. Purcell went on to put her coat in the hall closet.

"Nah, she knows he's just skinny." Jeff started after her. "Actually, she suspects you're giving him some secret growing formula, and one of these days she'll get it out of him what it is. Then she'll start giving it to me!"

Dale exhaled with exasperation. All he'd wanted was an invitation to dinner, not a big old chummy conversation. "If I'm eating at Jeff's," he said to hurry things along, "I better not make too much salad, huh?"

"Can I go outside and see if my new boots work?"

Matt piped up. "Anyway, I have to walk the dog. He's been in all day. We don't want him to do something disgusting, do we?"

They didn't have a dog, but Matt had peculiar ways of begging for one.

Their mom came back into the open kitchen area. "If you'll promise to stay on the grass, you may go outside. Don't ruin those soles, you hear?"

Matt plunked down on the dining-room floor to untie his shoes, singing, "Cross my heart . . . hope to die . . . stick a finger in my eye. . . ."

"How about it, Mom?" Dale asked, his tension building by the second.

"I better check with Meredith first. Would she be home yet?"

Oh no! She was heading straight for the phone.

Dale jerked around to get Jeff's eye, but he wasn't paying attention. He was down on the floor with Matt, playing with the Velcro boot tabs. By the time Jeff reacted to Dale's high-pitched squeak, she'd already punched the buttons.

"No!" Jeff shouted, leaping to his feet. "She's not there yet."

Too late! The phone, with the big blob of gum on it, was firmly pressed against his mother's ear and someone was at the other end.

Mrs. Purcell turned her back to the boys so she could hear better.

"Meredith? Cathy. Fine, how are you? Is this an official invitation—Dale over there for dinner tonight? I'm never sure."

Jeff started edging toward his jacket, but Dale went after him and got his neck in a death grip.

"Oh, I see." She swung around to look at Jeff, who had capital-letter guilt all over his face. "Oh, nice . . . well, it's a good thing I called. Sure, I'll send him home right away."

When she went to hang up the phone, the gum—the whole nasty green gob—stayed right where it stuck. Dale saw her wince, then frown, then feel around to see what was pulling her hair. He held his breath, but luck was with him and her fingers touched everything but the gum. He couldn't look at Jeff. He didn't dare, not with that big thing hanging right below his mother's ear, swinging like a spearmint cocoon.

"Did you forget you're going to a ball game tonight?" Mrs. Purcell said, speaking to Jeff. "Your dad's picking you up. Scram, now. Meredith wants you home."

"Oh, yeah, that's right!" His smile was pure relief as he wrestled free from Dale and snatched up his Levi's jacket. "Soooo—see you later—" He backed away fast. "Let me know how things come out—hah, hah!"

Dale opened the door and gave him a shove. "Thanks for nothing, fink," he said between clenched teeth. "Just wait!"

Right behind them came Matt, clomping along in the new boots, tugging on an imaginary leash. "Come on, Waggy, I'll take you for a walk." For the first time, Dale wished he had a dog that needed walking.

"MATTHEW DAVID!" came their mom's voice over the slamming of the door. "Did you park your gum on the phone? You get right back here!"

End of luck.

Dale bounded on up the steps. *He* hadn't put it there and that was the truth.

"I'll be doing homework," he called innocently from the top of the steps.

She must have calmed down and got the gum out of her hair, because she didn't go after Matt or him, either. The bathroom door slammed once; the next sound he heard was the music for the evening news, which meant his mom was back in the kitchen starting dinner.

A week ago she'd have lined them up for an inquisition, but getting the concert tickets from Richard had put her in an extra-mellow mood lately. The trouble was, no mood was good enough to deal with all those single women who were about to call. How could he have been so stupid? What was he going to do, anyway?

Dale settled down at his desk to stare at his homework. Maybe they'd luck out. Maybe "Blake," the mystery man, would call after all, and the two of them would hit it off. They'd end up talking about waterskiing or a book they'd read recently. It was possible. It happened to people that way. They'd have a date, get to liking each other, maybe even fall in love.

Later . . . only it wouldn't be the way it was when his dad was there. It would never be like that. He'd have to get used to someone new, but he thought he could do it. He remembered again how miserable his mom had been since summer and knew he wanted her to be happy. "Help!" he said aloud to his lonely room.

As if in answer, the phone rang. Dale hung tight to the edge of his desk until he heard her answer. He then crept in his stocking feet down to the landing, where he could hear her say, "You must have the wrong number."

She seemed to be listening, then she laughed. She didn't sound mad at all. In the end, she told someone "Good luck." He heard her hang up and walk back across the kitchen *singing*. Her voice was lilting, like Emmylou Harris's. "If We Make It Through December—" It was a Merle Haggard favorite of hers.

He stood listening a minute longer. He could smell hamburger frying, could hear the whirr of the can opener. It was strange, having everything seem so normal when it definitely wasn't. He tiptoed back up to his room. Lindsey could save him if she wasn't so late getting home from the gym. He'd have to tell her now. Maybe he could pay her a buck to grab the calls ahead of their mom, to screen them or something.

The phone again. Two in a row. He froze.

"Oh, hi, Meredith," his mom's voice floated up.

Dale let his body slump. Good old Meredith! She could talk forty minutes without a breath, though she'd just been on the phone a few minutes ago. He was saved. He could do his homework, watch TV, and catch Lindsey, all before she finished.

Dale was working on his second social studies question when he looked up to see his mom standing in the doorway with a crumpled newspaper page in her hand. The ad section!

"Start talking" was all she said.

Dale tried to swallow, but he couldn't.

"Did you really think this was going to work? An ad in the personals column? For your own mother? I'm so humiliated I could die. Meredith saw it and she's over there laughing her head off. All those people at work— I can't believe it! Advertising our phone number for any idiot to see. Dale, what made you do this? And don't tell me you didn't!"

He covered his face with his hands. "Yes, I did it. Jeff helped me."

"Oh no! Jeff, too? What were you thinking about?"

He shoved back his chair, wanting to cry, but mad, too. "I was thinking about you!" he yelled.

She blinked, wadded up the paper, stuffed it in his wastebasket. Her face was as red as he'd ever seen it.

"All right, if you're so concerned about me, you get to answer the phone. I want to hear you admit to whoever calls that *you* placed that ad, that your mother's furious, and that you're sorry to have been an inconvenience.

"DOWNSTAIRS THIS MINUTE!" she ordered.

Dale's eyes stung as he got to his feet. Everything had backfired. He was out seven dollars, and every single thing that could go wrong had gone wrong. The worst part was, his mom hated him. He could see it in her face. She hated the sight of him.

The next big humiliation was when Lindsey came home, all sweaty and tired, and had to hear the whole story from their mom. He was starting to feel like a criminal. Minutes later, his sister repeated it to her girlfriend over the phone, then again for Matt when he returned from "Anardick" with his sled dog. Lindsey and Matt thought it was hilarious until their mom threatened to strangle them if they didn't quit laughing. None of it was funny to Dale.

There were seventeen calls, by actual count, before the ten-o'clock news came on and things died down. Only two were men, one who sounded about ninety and another who wouldn't talk, just said, "Hmmmmmm, hmmmm." Dale was shaking with nerves and sick of apologizing, but his mother wouldn't let him take the phone off the hook or go to bed, either one.

"I hope you're learning a lesson" was absolutely all she'd say.

About ten fifteen she put on a New Age album she'd checked out of the library, made herself a bubble bath, and left him to face the phone calls alone.

The very next one was the whole reason for what he'd done. His stupid stunt would have cost him his mom *except* . . . the very next caller was Blake. Well, not really *Blake* because his name was John, but he sounded like an answer from heaven. With his mother out of earshot and the guy saying he had called in response to "the delightful ad in today's *Gazette*—in the personals," Dale vowed he wouldn't blow this chance, no matter what.

"The ad's for my mom," he admitted right off, "but I'm the one who ran it."

"Interesting," the man said. "I have a fifteen-year-old daughter who thinks I'm going to stay a bachelor forever.'' His laugh rang into the phone and Dale could almost see his face.

"My mother's in the bathtub right now—'' What was he going to say? "She's pretty mad at me, actually.''

Tell the truth came a voice from inside.

So he explained what he'd done and how he mightn't live to see the dawn if something good didn't come of it.

"How old are you, son?'' John asked, very upfront.

"Thirteen.''

"—and enterprising.'' The guy laughed again, like he was having the best time. "And your name is—''

"Dale. Dale Purcell.''

"Would you believe I've never done this before?'' John went on, sounding kind of embarrassed.

"Oh, me either, and I'm never going to again.''

"You know, my daughter Kelli has been putting clippings on my breakfast plate for two years now. She'd love to be a matchmaker. But something about this ad . . . well, it caught my fancy, made me curious. You should be commended if you wrote it yourself.''

"Jeff helped me some, but it was my idea.''

"Jeff's your brother?''

"No, my best friend. Matt's my brother, but he's just a little squirt."

"Well, how can we get you off the hook with your mom? Do you suppose you and she and Matt could meet Kelli and me for hamburgers tomorrow night? How about Wendy's?"

"On Highland Drive?"

"Right. Everybody like Wendy's?"

"The thing is—" Dale grabbed a breath. "I have a sister, too—Lindsey. There are three of us. Four if you count Waggy, who we always have to drag along. But he's imaginary so I guess you don't have to count him."

"That's quite a family you've got," said John, still sounding friendly in spite of roll call. "So what do you say? Think your mom would agree?"

All kinds of warning signals were flashing in Dale's head, but he knew what he was going to say before he said it: knew it, regretted it, said it anyway. "What time? I'll see if I can get her there. Lindsey's out of gymnastics at six on Fridays. Have to be after that."

"Say six thirty. Now, how will I know you? I mightn't recognize Waggy." He was chuckling away still, sounding like he'd never had so much fun in his life.

"I'll wear a purple baseball cap. It'll say 'The Jazz' on it in gold."

"Fine, so we're on for tomorrow night. If you

can't swing it, I'll at least have Kelli off my back, won't I?''

Dale couldn't think of anything else to say, so they thanked each other politely for the nice conversation and hung up.

He leaned back, grinning. If Blake—that is, *John*—was half as good as he sounded . . .

In a burst of optimism, Dale took the phone off the hook, climbed the stairs, and went to bed.

Later, when the house was dark, when he couldn't sleep, he slipped across the hall in his pajamas and left his essay, "My Life as Man of the House," in front of his mother's bedroom door. He'd added a note alongside the big red "A" at the top explaining that Mrs. Okimoto had read it to the class.

chapter 8

Friday morning at the Purcells' was as hectic as ever. Naturally Matt threw a fit when he couldn't wear his combat boots to school.

"Go outside and see for yourself," said Lindsey, forever trying to reason with him. "There isn't a cloud anywhere. Besides, the weatherman—"

"I hate the weatherman," Matt blubbered. "He lies!"

Mrs. Purcell was being very calm. For some reason she'd dressed earlier than usual, was wearing her executive-looking blue suit and striped blouse. Her heels tapped on the tile as she walked around shaking cinnamon sugar on everyone's toast. Dale figured it would have been easier to bring up Wendy's hamburgers if she were still in her bathrobe looking sleepy.

A minute later she poured herself some coffee and sat down at the counter next to Matt.

"No more fussing," she said as she patted him on the head. "If you remembered what we're going to do tonight after school, you'd be grinning so wide your face would split. I guess you've forgotten." She had Lindsey pass the milk, then started in on her cereal.

Matt dropped the sulking, sat up straight. "We still going to?"

Wish my life were that simple, thought Dale, watching a smile take over his little brother's face. When Matt was happy, his apple cheeks and electric eyes brightened the whole continent.

"Okay, smarty, what are you and Mom doing tonight?" Dale asked, hoping it wouldn't interfere with what he had in mind.

"We're going to the pet shop," Matt answered. He sneaked his toast along the counter and dipped it into his mother's coffee.

She moved her cup to the other side. "For now we're just looking."

"But maybe—" Matt went on, "if we see, you know, a dog—an' he isn't too big—"

"What's wrong with Waggy?" Dale asked. "How's he going to feel if you bring home a real dog?"

Matt's face clouded at once.

"Dale!" His mom scolded. "Do you ever think before you speak? Don't make things harder."

"Don't pay attention to stupids," Lindsey whispered to Matt. "Waggy and the new dog can play together, that's what's neat."

"Yeah," Matt agreed, curling his lip, a trick he'd picked up at school just that week. "I never listen to stupids."

Dale stared at the peanut butter he was spreading. He couldn't do anything right, even make breakfast conversation. So what had made him think, last night, that he could get the whole family to Wendy's? What had made him think he was going to solve his mom's problems by advertising in the first place? All he'd advertised was his own stupidity.

By seven forty-five Lindsey was running out of the house with her gym bag. A minute later Matt's ride came and tooted. As usual Dale and his mom would have some time to themselves before she had to catch the bus or get out the car, but today he wasn't looking forward to being alone with her.

After what seemed like a long, sticky interval, his mother swiveled sideways so she could face him across Lindsey's empty stool.

"I loved your essay," she said, surprising him. "I didn't know you could write so well."

He shrugged. "It was just an assignment."

"No, no, it was great. Funny, and so—something else. Special, I guess. You know, it kind of got to me."

Now he was the one grinning. As easily as Matt's, his mood had swung all the way from black to yellow.

"I'm sorry I was so mean last night," she went on. "I guess I forget I'm not the only one making adjustments around here. Dale, I want you to talk to me when you need to. You shouldn't have to wait for an English assignment to be able to say what you feel. Will you promise to let me in on your life a little?"

He nodded, laid a crust of toast on his plate. He wondered if she meant what she was saying, wondered how nice she'd be if she knew what else he'd done.

"Nonetheless, I hope you're up to answering the phone again tonight."

"I shouldn't have put that ad in the paper, but it didn't turn out . . . I mean . . . I didn't think you'd get so mad, honest."

"I'll get over it."

He nodded again.

"If we live on through till Sunday!" She belted out new words to her Merle Haggard favorite. Dale laughed. Their blues always sounded better sung to someone else's tune.

"You know what I want to do?" He draped his arms across Lindsey's stool, leaning close to his mom. "I want to take us all to Wendy's for hamburgers tonight. Can I?"

She started to shake her head no.

"Please? After the pet shop we could swing by the gym, get Lindsey. I have money from my birthday and I want to treat everybody. Come on, you got to let me."

She smiled. "Are you speaking as man of the house now or as my thirteen-year-old kid?"

"Both," he said, giving her his most intense eyes.

She stood and carried dishes to the sink. "All right, if you're sure you want to spend your money on hamburgers. I'm willing."

Dale smacked the counter with both hands. "Yahoo!" It was going to happen. A miracle! They'd all be at Wendy's when John showed up.

"I want you to know we also have a date Saturday night," she called over her shoulder as she went for her coat and purse, "just you and me."

Dale looked up from the dishwasher he was loading. "We do? How come?"

"I need a partner for the concert, don't I?"

"The Dwight Yoakam concert? What about Richard?"

"What about him?" she said, on her way back through the kitchen. "He gave *me* the tickets. And I'm asking you. Pretty rad, huh?"

"All right!" Dale shouted, swinging her around until she made him let go.

As soon as her car pulled out of the driveway, he was on the phone with Jeff. If he could just borrow five bucks now, he'd have it made.

chapter 9

With Matt doing doggy imitations and Lindsey changing into jeans in the backseat of the car, they still made it to Wendy's that night with ten minutes to spare. Good! It would take them that long to study the menu.

At the last minute, Dale gave the members of his family the once-over, trying to see them through a stranger's eyes. He liked his mom in the blue suit, though John might find her a smidge overweight. Lindsey, whose hair was still kinky and damp from the workout, was passable. Barely. Matt looked like any other kid, his clothes skewed around because he wouldn't tuck in. Half the time he forgot to zip up his coat, sometimes his pants. It drove their mom crazy.

Dale pulled down the visor mirror and adjusted his cap so "The Jazz" read straight across. He probably looked better than any of them. He'd taken a shower and changed clothes, used a drop of what had been his dad's cologne.

Another block and they were pulling into Wendy's parking lot. Everyone piled out. Suddenly, Dale's palms got sweaty and he found himself hanging back, though he knew he should be first in to look around. Why hadn't he asked John whether he wore glasses, was tall, short, bald, fat, or what? And what was he supposed to say if the two of them were already sitting there waiting? Oh lord!

He walked into Wendy's with his throat closing off, but from what he could see through the windows, they weren't there yet. It was still too early to be crowded.

Matt had to swing on the brass rails, as always, as the rest of them studied the menu on the wall. His mom decided on salad, period.

"No diet drink," she said, "but maybe I'll have coffee later."

"No fries?" Dale asked, knowing she was trying to save him money.

While Lindsey and Matt ordered, Dale stepped back to where he could see the eating area. An older woman sat by herself reading a book, three girls his age had their heads together by the windows. There were several couples, but he didn't see a single father-daughter combination.

When it came time to pay, Dale was a dollar twenty-five short and his mom had to help. Not bad, considering he was getting a Classic Burger, fries, and small drink for himself. As his mom made up the difference, it suddenly occurred to him that maybe they should have waited. Maybe John wanted to take them to dinner and they were doing a very rude thing by ordering ahead.

He could feel his face getting hot. How was he supposed to know what to do? All of a sudden, there were too many "if's." For all he knew, John could be some crazy joker who never once planned to show up. It was a little odd how he laughed so much. Maybe the laugh wasn't nervousness. Maybe he didn't have any intention of meeting them at Wendy's!

"Dale, take off your cap, you're inside," his mother said, breaking into his thoughts as they chose a table. She emptied Matt's tray and handed it to Dale, along with Lindsey's and hers. "Your cap?" she said, nodding at it.

"Oh, I'll just wear it."

"You will not." She reached up and took it off him.

He put it back on. "I didn't comb my hair." He

glanced over at the girls and hoped she'd think something else. She didn't. She just pulled a comb out of her purse and told him to go visit the "Men's" first if he was so sensitive.

Off he went, casing the parking lot on his way. He should have asked what kind of car John had. *Don't tell me you're driving next year's Honda Prelude. Mercedes, you say? Sure, I know a Mercedes.*

He combed his hair in about one second, hurried back. He insisted on putting the cap up on their tiny square table, but Lindsey, true to form, elbowed it off with a sarcastic "Excuuuuse me."

He picked it up, absently clapped it back on his head. So far he hadn't had a bite of dinner and everyone else was eating away.

When his mom saw him wearing it again, she said, "Watch it, Buster, you're pushing me."

So the cap ended up on his knees where John would never see it. By then he wasn't a bit hungry, but his nervous pinpricks and itches numbered in the thousands. Why hadn't he ordered a drink more his size? He'd never choke the burger down.

Several minutes later, John and his daughter walked in. Dale knew who they were immediately. The daughter might be two years older, but, with her bright-pink face, she looked as miserable as he felt. He figured she'd turn around and run if anyone said "Boo."

80

They were both taller than average, on the lanky side. John had some gray hair, tan crinkles around his eyes, and was wearing jeans. His white shirt was open at the throat and three pens stuck up out of a plastic pocket protector. Like a terrified but well-trained detective Dale took it all in. This man was older than the "Blake" they'd imagined, but he wasn't bad.

The two of them were inside the dining area only seconds before John's eyes lit on Dale's group and John knew who Dale was, too.

Quickly Dale hauled up his cap, pretending to look at it.

In three steps John was at their table, extending his hand for a shake. "Dale, good to see you!"

"Oh, hi," Dale said, too scared to stand up. They shook hands, Dale aware of how limp his own hand must feel. Lindsey and his mom looked on in surprise.

"Is this your family?" John asked. He swallowed hard enough for Dale to hear, though his eyes were still enjoying their private joke.

"Yeah, this is my mom and Lindsey and Matt. That's everybody." Then, remembering, "—and this is John." If he'd heard John's last name, he'd forgotten it.

"John Delancey. It's a pleasure to meet you."

Now Dale's mother looked really confused.

"You're one of Dale's teachers?"

"No," he answered, "we just got acquainted the other day." He turned and pulled his daughter up beside him, told them her name was Kelli, with an *i*, and that she was a sophomore at Viewmont High. Still blushing, she gave them a trace smile, showing a full set of iron on her teeth.

"We've been to the pet shop," Matt volunteered, his eyes all sparkly. "I'm getting a dog."

"Are you?" John said. "Well, that'll be pretty exciting, won't it?"

Mrs. Purcell laughed and held up her hands. "For now we're just looking. Shopping around, right, Matt?"

"Kelli, why don't you order for us?" John said, sending his daughter to get in line. "I'll have my usual." He turned to their mom. "I know you weren't expecting company, but would we be in any real trouble if the two of us pulled up a table and joined you?"

She raised her eyebrows, looked across at Dale and Lindsey. "Okay with you kids?"

Dale and Lindsey nodded that it was okay. Matt was the one who was frowning. He pointed at John's feet. "Watch out, you're standing on him. You're right where Waggy wants to be."

John jumped away. "Clumsy of me! Sorry, Waggy, I didn't see you there."

Matt wriggled around, came up with a smile that was as good as an invitation.

"That Waggy!" Dale's mom said. "Matt usually leaves him in the car."

Dale got up and helped slide another square table up to where he'd been sitting. Once everyone was settled, John was next to his mom and right across from him. Kelli would have the spot on the end. So far so good. When John left to pay, Dale jumped up to get more ketchup so his mother wouldn't have a chance to ask who this guy was, for crying out loud. He could tell she really wanted to.

A few minutes later they were all chatting away, not exactly like old friends, but close. After telling them he was a city planner for one of the newly incorporated areas, John actually got Dale's mom to talk about her job as a legal secretary at the courthouse. The bat invasion had been on the news, and they all had to laugh about the weird measures being taken by the county commissioner to get rid of their "bats in the belfry."

"We're not having fire drills at the courthouse these days, we're having bat drills," Dale's mom told John.

A little later, Kelli, in a shy voice, told Dale she was trying out for a play, but didn't think she'd get a part. Dale said he was almost positive she would. Lindsey spent most of her time trying to keep Matt from butting into the adults' conversation.

Actually it was kind of nice, all of them together, and Dale was beginning to relax. So far they'd gotten away with everything. He wasn't positive, but he thought John was starting to like them a little, especially his mom, who could be a lot of fun when she wanted to. The more they talked, the more mellow things got. Dale was trying to see how he could steer the conversation to boating and waterskiing—just to find out—when Matt took a swing at Lindsey for bossing him too much. He missed her, naturally, but he knocked over his orange drink and ruined everybody's good mood.

Luckily he'd finished most of it, so it was mainly ice that slid across the table and onto the floor. Right away he set up a yowl and insisted on having seconds. It was all pretty embarrassing, but John got extra napkins and cleaned things up while their mother kept saying what a nuisance, what a pity, and "No, Matthew, you may not have another drink!"

"Looks like Waggy licked most of it up," John said. "He really likes orange drink."

"HE HATES IT!" Matt shouted at the top of his lungs.

Dale wiped his hot hands on his cords. He should have warned John that Waggy was copyrighted as far as Matt was concerned.

At that point their mother apparently decided it was time they leave. A certain look around her mouth said, plain as day, "Come on, kids, the fun's over. I'm tired, let's go."

"I'll have coffee at home," she said when Dale pointed out she'd never ordered any.

Dale himself felt terrible. They'd had less than twenty minutes together; it was hardly a beginning. John felt bad, too, Dale could tell, though he was trying to keep up Kelli's spirits by goofing around and stealing her fries.

"You'll have to excuse us," Mrs. Purcell said as she stood and put on her coat. "Matt's had a lot of excitement today."

John stood up, too. "Of course, but I'm sorry you can't stay."

Their mother was zipping Matt's coat when the dreaded question came out. "You know?" She straightened, frowned. "Neither of you has explained how you happen to know each other. Do you live in our neighborhood?" she asked John, innocent as anything.

He looked at Dale, smiled, looked back at her. "Sure you want to know? Why don't I say we just, well . . . got our heads together the other night."

Dale's mother gave John a questioning look, then turned to pin *him* with one of the same. Oh no, she was putting the pieces together! He could tell. She was going to hit the ceiling, right there in front of God and everybody at Wendy's.

"I don't think I like this," she said, spacing her words.

John sobered in a hurry. "You're right. I don't blame you. Dale and I got acquainted when I called your house last night. You couldn't come to the phone right then, so we had a minute to talk. He's a fine boy."

She knotted her belt, jerked it tight, grabbed Matt's hand.

"Wait, please," John said. "This meeting at Wendy's was my idea. I happen to be a country music nut myself. Ask Kelli. Right, Kelli?"

Kelli wasn't saying anything. She just sat there trying to make herself disappear, same as Dale.

"Lindsey, Dale, come this minute or I'm leaving without you!"

John spread his hands, a hopeless look on his face. "I'm going to feel pretty foolish if you walk out of here mad."

"That doesn't concern me."

Oh Mom, please!

John went right along with them to the door, holding it open for their mom, waiting for her to go first, but still talking. "I don't know what the *C* stands for yet. I don't even know your name. This is pretty awful, you know that?''

Mrs. Purcell made a beeline for the car, pulling Matt, with John striding next to her and the rest trailing, all but Kelli, who'd had sense enough to stay put.

"I'm beginning to think *C* stands for Commodity!" she said. "That's how you both make me feel. I'm not up for auction. I don't need to meet a man, is that clear, Dale? I loved your father and I wonder how you could want to replace him so soon—or at all.''

Somehow they all got into the car. John went around to close the door on the driver's side, then stood there outside the window, hands on the roof, a disappointed, perplexed look on his face.

Suddenly his mother's head went down on the wheel, and all the stiffening inside her seemed to collapse.

"What's wrong?" Matt asked, sounding scared.

The next thing Dale knew, his mother was rolling down the window and apologizing. "I'm sorry. Please, tell your daughter—really—I'm not myself right now. I haven't been myself—''

John didn't say anything at first. He just stood there shivering in his shirt sleeves and nodding.

"I take it you lost your husband. How long's it been?" he asked before she turned the key.

"Two and a half years."

"Too soon," John said like an expert. "Things will ease."

Then John, alias Blake, backed off, waved, gave Dale a special salute, and returned to Wendy's.

chapter 10

After John, things went from bad to worse, as the saying goes. The Purcell family made it through December, all right, thanks to Grandma and Grandpa Sherwood, who sent them plane tickets for Christmas. Thanks also to their mother, who talked them into making most of their presents.

Fortunately, Dale had learned to build picture frames in his shop class. *Un*fortunately, that meant everyone they knew ended up with snapshots under glass for gifts.

Here's Matt, hugging a snowman. (Eight-by-ten-inch medium-oak-stained frame.)

Here's Lindsey, poised on the balance beam in her lavender tights. (Same size, mahogany-stained frame.)

Dale himself, in racing position on his outgrown BMX. (Glossy black.)

The grandparents liked the photographs better than anything else they got for Christmas. At least that's what they said.

If you judged by the smiles in those pictures, you'd think the Purcells were a happy family like any other—each doing his or her own regular, happy thing. What didn't show up in the snapshots was 1) the plugged toilet that was waiting for a paycheck so they could call a plumber; 2) the bills piled up on the kitchen desk; 3) the Christmas notes their mom wrote but never mailed because of postage; and, 4)—rock bottom—their mom sitting at the dining-room table staring out at a blizzard. As she'd done one day for an hour. Without moving.

When Dale finally asked what she was doing, she said she was storing up energy and please not to bother her. She reminded him of one of those plugged-in appliances that has only so many minutes of electrical charge. He guessed "fizzling out" was what she was trying to prevent.

Other facts of life not obvious inside Dale's picture frames were the oatmeal breakfasts they had instead of Honey-Puffs and the awful haircuts they were getting from Meredith. She was taking a class in Restorative Art, learning how to make dead people look natural. The Purcells had become her "victims," as Jeff pointed out with big guffaws. The weird cuts didn't matter to *him*. His black hair was so curly even Meredith couldn't ruin it. But Dale's hair was brown, straight, and stubborn. When her scissors made stairsteps on the back of his head, he was in trouble for weeks.

On top of everything else, Matt had been sick during most of January and February. He'd stayed home so many days, their mom's job was in jeopardy and she had to find a daytime sitter.

Matt loved it, of course. On sick days he could watch *Dinosaucers* every morning and *Sesame Street* every afternoon. In between, he'd talk Mrs. Dearborn into reading his favorite books as he snuggled beside her, sucking on the peppermints she carried in her needlepoint bag.

"She buys them just for me," he'd boast to Dale. He didn't know the baby-sitter's fee was costing his mom a mint. It was no concern of *his*, all the antibiotics they charged at the pharmacy.

Dale got so nervous about what was happening to their family, he broke out in the worst zits of his life. Three major explosions in one week. Even with Clearasil, he looked like a candidate for clown school. The only comfort was noticing two serious zits on Lizette's cheek the one time they were close enough to say "hi."

The last week in February Dale rode along in the car with his mom and Matt to the doctor's—mostly out of boredom. Lindsey had forgotten a signed permission slip for a meet, so they had to stop by the gym first. Once there, Dale decided to stay. Hanging out with the gymnasts would be twice the kick as waiting at the doctor's.

"You sure now?" his mom asked as she pulled to the curb in front of Valley View Gymnastics.

"I'm sure." Dale got out, then had to grab the door when a whipping wind threatened to rip it off.

His mom leaned across from the driver's side. "We'll be two hours, at least, so wait inside if Lindsey's finished first. The cold's bitter."

"Okay. Hey, Matt—" Dale shouted into the back seat, "remember what I told you about mercury. Don't bite down on the thermometer this time."

Matt pulled a sucker out of his mouth long enough to say, "I won't."

They waved and drove off, Dale listening to the muffler that was sure to get them arrested someday.

Inside the converted-warehouse gymnasium, he left the permission slip with the secretary, crossed the lobby, and went on into the gym.

Everything looked different. Of course, he hadn't been there for a year. On his right, the advanced gymnasts were chalking up and doing routines on the bars.

In the left corner of the gym the younger kids skipped in a circle, crossing and uncrossing their arms like ballet dancers, everyone barefooted and in rainbow leotards.

He didn't see Lindsey at first, so he just stood there zipping and unzipping his parka and kind of enjoying the chalky, sweaty smell of the place. Finally, spotting *him* from the top of a beam, Lindsey smiled and gave a little wave her coach wouldn't notice.

Dale stepped across the mats to a folding chair near the wall and sat down. Optionals and compulsories on the beam were sacred stuff according to Lindsey.

"Tighten up, Andrea!" Jared yelled from where he sat on a stool in baggy gray sweats. He was studying every move his girls made. Then, "Touch your ears, Darcey!"

"No, no, noooooo!" He jumped up and halted the next routine. "Are we into wasting our time today, Toni? Is that what we're into?"

Dale would have died, but the gymnasts took everything their coach dished out.

When it was Lindsey's turn to demonstrate, she executed what seemed to Dale a perfect backflip, landing squarely on her feet with a little dip and graceful arms. He found himself grinning. He'd never seen her do anything *that* smooth before, but Jared yelled at her, too. "Come on, watch that chin. Remember what we talked about?"

Dale studied the floor, figuring she'd be embarrassed. Seconds later, sneaking a look, he realized she wasn't even aware of him.

"Better!" Jared told her. "Much better."

Dale was used to seeing his sister doing "stomachs" and "hamstrings" at home, but it came as a shock that she was developing—what did his mom call it?—*finesse.* She might be one of the tiniest in the class, but as the hour went on, he could see she was also the best. The other girls had the same pink, perspiring faces and tied-back hair as Lindsey, but they just didn't get into it the way she did.

Later, watching her tear down the runway to the springboard, hit the horse, go vaulting over, Dale was sure she'd completely forgotten he was there. She was concentrating totally on what she was doing. She had to, he figured, if she didn't want to kill herself.

"Great landing there!" Jared called to her.

Dale began to feel funny. How many times had he said the words "stupid Olympic potential"? For two years now he'd been thinking Lindsey ought to pack it in, like, "Look, you've had your lessons. There are two other kids in this family, you know?" At least once a week he'd lie on his bed plotting how they'd spend the extra three hundred bucks if Lindsey would only slip on the ice and break her leg.

Today, seeing how she stuck to that puny little four-inch beam, he was actually impressed.

It was six thirty when the gym cleared and kids of all ages bunched into the lobby to wait for rides. Surrounded by the gymnasts' clatter, obviously an outsider, Dale stood there towering over everyone else. Fervently he wished their Ford wagon would be the next car to pull into the circle.

"How'd you like it?" Lindsey asked when she came out of the gym. She was still breathing hard, as if she'd rushed getting dressed.

"It was okay."

"I was terrible today," she said, "really. I couldn't do anything."

Dale figured she was fishing for a compliment, so he didn't say anything.

"Where'd they have to go?" she asked, handing Dale her gym bag so she could comb her hair.

"Who?"

"Mom. Where'd she and Matt go? She said I shouldn't ride home with the Brannigans tonight."

"Matt had to have another shot."

"Oh, ouch. I'd hate to be him." She poked her comb back into her bag.

A quarter hour later, they were still waiting, the last in the lobby.

Lindsey's coach and another trainer came out of

the gym, yakking away.

"Ma petite," Jared said, tapping her on the head as he walked by. He winked at Dale. "She's gonna be a star, this one."

Lindsey beamed. "He's really great. I was wishing he'd demonstrate today so you could see him, but he never did."

Another ten minutes went by before the secretary came out of the office with her coat and purse. "Are you sure someone's coming for you? I'm sorry, but I have to lock up."

"Mom's at the doctor's," Dale explained, "but we can wait outside just as well." He started for the door. "Come on, Linds, grab your stuff."

It was plenty dark after the gym lights were cut—with only the Valley View sign glowing in the window. But the cold was worse than the dark. They'd freeze if they had to stand there very long. Remembering his promise to wait inside, Dale frowned and jammed his hands deeper into his pockets.

"You think she forgot us?" Lindsey asked, yanking her cap down to her eyebrows. She danced to his other side, where she'd be blocked from the wind, then tipped back her head to see him. "Where's your cap?"

"Home, where else?" Dale shivered and looked past her at the long line of red taillights sliding down the freeway ramp. Weird how the cars appeared to be floating on their own billowy exhaust. Their family was going down the tube the same way and none of them knew what to do about it.

Beside him, Lindsey continued to chatter away about whatever came into her head. *She* wasn't worried. "I'd give anything for some Kentucky Fried Chicken!" she was saying at the moment.

Dale's own head was spinning. Suddenly he felt old and responsible, and he didn't want to be either. It still bugged him, Lindsey's lessons taking so much of their money, but after two hours at the gym, he agreed with their mom: She had to stay with gymnastics. She was good. Like Jared said, she might even be a star someday.

"Maybe I could get a job," he muttered, more to himself.

"Where *is* she?" Lindsey stamped her feet again. "I bet she forgot. What do we do if she doesn't show?"

"I guess we walk."

"Five miles? Oh, help! Say, do you have any gum on you? My stomach's growling like crazy."

She was also *shaking* like crazy. Dale reached down and zipped her parka the rest of the way to her chin, then rubbed his ears until his hands hurt from the cold. Ears, faces, hands—they'd turn blue before they starved.

"Who can we call?" Lindsey asked. "How about Meredith?"

"You mean if we had a quarter?"

A blast of ice crystals made them duck into each other.

"Or if we had a 7-Eleven," Lindsey moaned.

"You know Mom didn't forget us, she's just late again. She stopped for gas or something."

They didn't talk for a minute, long enough for Dale to wonder who he was trying to protect this time.

Suddenly Lindsey started in on the worries he didn't think she had, and most were the same as his—how they never had any money, how Matt's bronchitis had gone on so long, how everything was broken down, how the yukky winter weather pushed up the bills. She also told him how embarrassed she was when the coach suggested her leotards might be too small. Her words sounded funny coming through stiff lips, but he listened.

"Mostly," she said, "it's Mom. I really get nervous about her."

"Me, too."

"You think she's sort of . . . you know . . . depressed?"

"Probably. Wouldn't you be?"

Lindsey didn't answer, but her breath came out in a big, steamy gush.

"It's my fault. I should quit gymnastics. I've been thinking about it. I told Jared I might once, but he said, 'Over my dead body.' "

"You talked about our family to *him*?"

"Yeah, and don't call me a stool pigeon!" She pulled herself up an inch. "I have rights, too, you know."

Dale stared back, realizing that his dumb little sister was growing up. She had her own world. He might have hugged her right then, but he didn't. Instead, his hand snaked out and gave her a light slap on the cheek.

"Stop that!" she yipped.

Mom or no mom, Dale decided a minute later, they couldn't just stand there.

"Let's go," he said, taking the gym bag out of Lindsey's hand and hoisting the strap onto his shoulder. "Mom will figure it out. She'll find us if we walk along Eighth Street."

Lindsey gave him one of her big-eyed looks, but she stepped off the curb when he did.

It was icy getting across the street and dark enough to be scary, but a sidewalk began again when they got beyond the freeway cut. They hurried down a block of low, crouching houses and sheds, half of them unlighted although it was dinnertime. Dale knew this wasn't a safe part of the city, but what was he supposed to do? Tonight they were on their own and that's all there was to it.

They passed a printing place, a boarded-up café, a pawn shop, their footsteps noisy over patches of ice. If they came to a grocery or a drugstore, they'd go in and warm up a minute. His cheeks and ears were already going numb.

Just then two men came out of a dim place called The Pub, the warm, beery air escaping around them. The first guy noisily cleared his throat. The other one scratched a lighter to get a cigarette going, then swore when it didn't work. Sure enough, Lindsey's hand was right there working its way into Dale's pocket. He grabbed hold and held on tight, wondering what she'd be doing right now if he hadn't been at the gym.

They crunched across the icy ridges of an alley, where they had to steady each other to keep from falling.

At the end of the next block, Dale swung around to check the traffic. The street was busy enough, but did he have the nerve to hitchhike? His mom wouldn't stick up her thumb in a million years, but his dad had told stories about running away when he was fourteen. Nothing bad had happened to him except for falling asleep while some woman driver was lecturing him. She got so mad she took him to a police station and let them send him home.

After another prolonged blast of cold, Dale made up his mind.

"Catch," he said, tossing the gym bag to Lindsey.

He stepped to the curb and put up his thumb,

blinking into the lights of the very next car. "Keep up with me," he shouted back to her.

"I'm not getting in any stranger's car," she screamed. "Listen to me, Dale, I'm not!"

"Shut up and come on! I can't feel my ears. They're gonna drop off!"

Walking backward the way he'd seen people do, he hooked his thumb for every set of headlights. The cars passed him like he wasn't there. Didn't anyone care? Couldn't they see how cold he was without hat and gloves?

He was having a whole avalanche of second thoughts when Lindsey, who still hadn't moved, set up one of her horrifying howls.

Dale gritted his teeth. If she didn't stop, he'd drag *her* out on the curb. Cars would stop for a girl.

Suddenly he heard someone call his name. Dale swung around. Too late. A big, square four-by-four was right there blinding him. For a moment traffic was so thick he couldn't see or hear anything else.

"Dale! Over here!" it came again.

Jeff's voice! Where was he? A truck lumbered by, grinding down through its gears, but in a second's space he caught a glimpse of Jeff's Toyota at the opposite curb. There was a long blast on a horn. Jeff and his mom! A second later he could see she had the window down and was motioning them to cross over.

Lindsey spotted the car, too, and was suddenly whooping at the top of her lungs, thrilled to be rescued.

Laughing with relief, Dale ran back, grabbed Lindsey's sleeve so she wouldn't dive straight into the traffic, and tore with her across Eighth.

"Are we lucky to find you!" Meredith exclaimed as they climbed into the backseat over Jeff. "I've been up and down the frontage road, all over the place. Your mom's car broke down."

"I knew it!" Dale said. "I knew something happened to her! Where is she?"

"On Main Street at that Ford place. Lost the clutch and had to be towed. On a night like this. Push up that heat, Jeff . . . and share the cookies, my gosh!"

Jeff passed an opened bag back between the seats.

"Hey, man, were you thumbing?" Jeff asked Dale with what sounded like respect in his voice. "Looked like you were thumbing. Come on, is that what you were doing?"

Dale closed his eyes and pressed three ginger-snaps against the roof of his mouth until they dissolved. "You might say that," he answered thickly.

"Now listen up." Meredith poked Jeff on the near shoulder. "Anyone who tells Cathy we saw Dale hitchhiking gets to spend a night with me in Casket

City. She's got enough on her mind. You understand?"

"Not Casket City!" wailed Jeff in mock horror. "Not 'the shop'!"

"You better believe it!"

Dale and Lindsey exchanged grins as Jeff's mom laid on the horn to move someone over. She might be weird as Hallowe'en, but she was true blue. She was definitely someone a person could count on.

chapter 11

"Everybody's Had the Blues" became their mother's theme song for the entire week after the car broke down. She hummed it in the bathtub, while she was dusting, folding clothes, staring off. Shoveling the drive with Dale one frosty night, wailing out the opening line, she'd cut a path straight back to Nashville. All they'd needed was a harmonica.

There was something else going on at the Purcells' besides the blues. Matt, after being sick and inside so long, had reverted to playing like a preschooler. He made tents, dressed Lindsey's dolls, drank his juice from his old tippie cup. One more thing to worry about, thought Dale.

His latest kick was playing with the huge trunkful of red, yellow, blue, and green blocks that had belonged to each of them in turn.

As their dad had done for Lindsey and him, Dale went to the garage and carried in the four-by-eight-foot plywood sheet they used as a foundation. Laid flat on the carpet, the board would stay until Matt got tired of building doctors' offices and gyms and fast-food takeouts.

"Makes our living room look like a stupid playpen," Dale had grumbled at the time.

"It's okay," his mom insisted. "Matt needs to play with his old toys once in a while, so don't make him feel ashamed."

In his heart Dale understood. He'd never let Jeff catch him playing with blocks, but he wouldn't say no if Matt needed help on the skyscrapers.

One day he came home to find that his brother had laid out the entire floor plan of Smith's Co-op. And with amazing accuracy.

"Over here's where you find the caramel apples—" Matt had said when Dale asked for a tour, "and here's the aisle for dog food." His plump fingers patted a yellow block he said was the popcorn machine. He crab-walked to the other side of the store. "And toys are all over here."

"Three aisles for toys instead of one?" Dale said with a grin. "Neat."

That day Dale had made Matt a scale-sized shopping cart out of a strawberry basket and Lego wheels. When Lindsey suggested that Matt cut food and soap pictures out of magazines—for signs—Matt had two more days of fun labeling the aisles, filling his cart, and checking out.

It was Friday afternoon when Dale told Jeff on the school bus that he had things to do at home. "Chores and stuff. I'll call you later, okay?"

The truth was that he'd promised to show Matt what *he* used to build when he was little.

The night before, getting ready, they'd wrecked Smith's Co-op. It was great fun, though Matt had ended up with a coughing fit from laughing so hard. Things got pretty wild when the demolition crew threw lemon pies all over the bakery, then went sliding through the meringue, crashing into racks and knocking over displays. One of the hard-hat guys got stuck in the pretzel barrel and never did get out.

When the doorbell rang Saturday morning, Dale and Matt were already on their knees laying out the model city they'd decided to name Century 21.

Dale's heart sank, figuring it was Jeff. It wasn't. It was "Blake"—John Delancey—with his coat collar up and a brown paper bag in his hands.

"Am I interrupting anything?" he asked in the same jovial voice Dale remembered. "I'm too late for breakfast, but how about lunch?"

"Hi! Come on in," Dale said, standing back and laughing. He'd had a hunch John was going to show up on their doorstep someday and here he was.

"Is your mother home?"

"No . . . oh, heck!" Dale was so excited he couldn't think straight. "Where'd Mom go, Matt?"

"She's getting streaks in her hair," Matt answered. "Who's there?"

John definitely looked disappointed. "I should have called. But I was in your neighborhood—"

"Come in and wait," Dale suggested. "She's never long."

John's mustache wiggled as he tried to make up his mind about staying, but he followed Dale inside.

"Well, I don't have a lot of time. Look—" He opened up the sack he was carrying. "I had to go to Kelli's school bazaar last night and ended up with all these wholewheat groundhogs. I mean, what's a guy like me going to do with a dozen groundhogs?"

Matt bounded out of the living room. "Is it Groundhog Day again?"

John chuckled. "No, that was a month ago. That's why they were pushing these critters. Or maybe they're some wholesome new variety of Easter bunny. Beats me. What do you think?" He pulled out a brown, plastic-wrapped bun decorated with raisin eyes and frosting whiskers.

Matt agreed they looked more like groundhogs. "But we don't care what they are," he assured John. "We'll eat 'em!"

"Great! They're yours." John handed over the bag. "I'm allergic to groundhog anyway."

By then he'd noticed the blocks and asked what Matt's project was going to be when he finished. Dale realized he was just being polite, but maybe— if he got interested—he'd end up staying until their mom came home. He remembered Wendy's with a sick stomach, but it wasn't *his* fault this time and there mightn't be another chance.

"Why don't you wait awhile?" Dale said in his firmest voice. "Matt's been sick a lot and has had to stay home, but he loves showing people what he's building."

John glanced at his watch, then unbuttoned his coat and slung it over the banister the way nearly everyone did who came to their house. A minute later he was down on the living-room floor studying Dale's pencil sketch of Century 21 and nodding when he recognized things.

"You and Matt are in a partnership on this, I take it."

"Yeah, sort of—" Dale answered. He could feel the red creep into his ears and wondered what John would think of a thirteen-year-old playing with blocks. He hoped he'd just think he was baby-sitting.

"Airport's over there," John said, pointing to the runway where Matt's 747 was parked. "And what's this?"

"Waggy's doghouse!" Matt shouted in their faces.

Dale winced. The doghouse was more elaborate than the airline terminal.

"And look over here," Matt insisted. "Waggy's dog run goes all along the runway. Miles and miles, but he's a sled dog so he likes to run."

"I couldn't talk him out of that," Dale said apologetically.

"Waggy doesn't mind the noise?" John asked.

"Nope. He's used to it. He races the planes for exercise."

John nodded. "If anything, a city plan should be practical. I can see how a runway and a dog run would kind of . . . naturally . . . end up next to each other like this."

Matt gave them one of his world-class smiles. "That's what *I* said!"

Suddenly Dale remembered what it was John did for a living. Of course! He'd know all about city planning. Here they'd created a new city for a new century and an expert was sitting right across the board from them.

Dale straightened up to say, "John's a city planner, Matt, did you remember that?"

"Huh-uh."

John had to laugh. "If I'm not on the phone or at the computer, I do what you're doing . . . sometimes I use blocks myself. Or models to scale, to illustrate sizes and shapes of buildings, malls, parking lots."

"All *right*!" Matt said with big eyes. "So . . . we still need a video shop and a car place. An' Dale says a bank, and *I* say a shoe store. We started to build a railroad, but we got in a fight—"

Before long John had his sleeves rolled up, was bending over the board and showing them how *he*'d go about planning a whole new city if he ever got so lucky.

First he explained the "linear plan," which would work best if a city were built along a river—like on the Mississippi. That one was easy. They used a long red shoestring for the river.

"Or you might choose the radial plan."

Matt fished more blocks out of the trunk and shoved them toward John, who continued talking.

"Washington, D.C., is an example. We'll let this round piece be the Capitol building at the center. All the 'spokes' that come out from it are streets— here, and here—"

Matt watched with fascination as John laid out the civic center of a city whose heart was a wagon wheel.

"There's also the gridiron plan, as it's called." John looked up to see if they were following him, and Dale nodded. "Very popular in America, where the cities are new compared to what you'd find in the rest of the world. Take Salt Lake City in Utah. Streets were planned at ninety-degree angles, blocks laid out in squares—" Dale helped him make a grid of blocks. "Works great on the flats, but watch out for hills."

Matt was by then lying on his stomach, his head propped on two fists. "Our Century 21 is like the gridiron, huh?" he said.

"Exactly! Good observation." John patted him on the head and Matt squirmed with pleasure.

Half an hour later they were still at it, with all three of them laying out zones with blocks—blue for the civic area, red for the commercial area, a snaky green freeway to serve as a major traffic link. It was a phone call from Jeff that broke things up and left Matt groaning.

"I really have to go," John said when Dale came back from the phone. "Too bad. Time flies when you're having fun, doesn't it?"

"Yeah," Matt agreed, his mouth twisting to one side.

John stood, got back into his coat, hooked his scarf around his neck.

For a minute he looked kind of sad, as if he hated

to leave all the fun. "Thanks, you guys. Keep on, you're doing a great job. You'd probably have had Century 21 finished if I hadn't poked my nose in."

"Nooooooo," wailed Matt, who was now hanging on to the stair rails. "Do you have to go? I want you to stay."

John grinned, mussed his hair. "How about if I promise to come back sometime?"

Matt pouted, but finally nodded that would be all right.

"Dale," John said, turning to him, "I really do have to run. But how are things going? Is your mom okay?"

"She's fine." No way was he going to tell him how things really were!

"She wrote me a nice thank-you note for the Christmas fruit basket and I just wanted to . . . well, be in touch mostly."

Dale followed John to the door, saying, "I'll tell her. She never takes this long at the beauty parlor, but it's been ages since she went, so maybe her lady had a big job." He shrugged, hoping his disappointment didn't show too much.

"Do you want her to call you?" he asked John at the last minute. "I could take your number. I know she'd call."

"No, that's okay."

"It wouldn't be any trouble, honest."

"Thanks anyway," John said as he waved. "See you later."

Dale stood at the door and watched as John/Blake went down the walk to his truck. He hated good-byes, really hated them. What made it worse was knowing they were sometimes final.

chapter 12

"Have a party!" Dale crooned to the bathroom mirror in imitation of Elvis Presley. He'd just showered and changed clothes, and was combing his hair.

Meredith Ellis had invited their whole family over, something she hadn't done since she started mortician's college. They were, in fact, due at Jeff's in less than an hour. All except Matt, who was going for movies to his best friend's house, now that he was off medicine and feeling better.

What Dale and Jeff knew—and Dale's mother didn't—was that Meredith had planned everything to help get Dale's mom out of the dumps where she'd been for two and a half long, dreary months.

They were well into March when a finger of morning sun glinting off the sugar bowl made their mother smile. "Kids," she said, "I think winter's nearly over."

He'd known exactly what she was talking about, and it wasn't just the weather.

The spring thaw had helped, and sunny days brought out the daffodils, but the turnaround actually began when Jeff's dad showed up one night and fixed their toilet. Without being asked. He'd stayed an extra hour eating pie and griping about how much alimony it took to keep Meredith in school.

Also that week, a postcard picture of a glacier arrived with an Alaskan postmark. "Wouldn't want to water-ski in *this* lake," Richard had scrawled on the back, "but wish you were along for the sights."

Dale grinned remembering how Matt had snatched it up for yet another "Ardick" show-and-tell. Their mom had pointed out that, geographically, that particular glacier was too far south to qualify as "Ardick," but Matt didn't care. He and Waggy, magnificent Huskie, weren't fussy about things like latitude.

Now, with Lindsey pounding on the bathroom door, Dale gave his hair another spraying to get it to do what it was supposed to. Thanks to the new look being featured by morticians, he was a real standout at school.

Dale and Jeff had been skating in front of Jeff's only twenty minutes when what appeared to be a long, gold limousine came driving up Peruvian. It slowed. Dale, who'd never seen anything quite like it, swooped to the gutter and braked his board. The window slid down, the driver flashed them a smile, then pulled the huge thing right into the Ellises' driveway.

"Is that a hearse?" Dale asked, aghast.

"A coach, dummy." Jeff leaped off his board and tossed it on the grass.

Dale swallowed. The driver, with his blond hair and mustache, looked plenty friendly, but having a hearse that close gave Dale the creeps even if it hadn't come for him.

"That's Christopher," Jeff explained. "He goes to school with Mom."

The boys waited until whatever it was glided to a stop. A second later the man got out and walked around to the hatchback. Noiselessly, he extracted a red-and-white flower arrangement.

"Meredith home?" he asked, like the arrival of a funeral coach was as ordinary as the paper delivery. He was wearing Levi's but his top half looked more like ceremony: coat, shirt, tie.

116

Seeing how Dale was staring, he said, "You're not embarrassed to have me park here, are you? It'll soon be dark."

"Heck no, not me," said Dale, his voice breaking.

"Want me to get Mom?" Jeff offered.

"Sure, if it's not too much trouble."

The boys raced each other to the house.

"Dale!" Jeff grabbed him inside the door. "He's single! And morticians make a lot of money. How about him and your mom?"

"You kidding?" Dale squeaked.

Jeff shushed him, glanced over his shoulder. "How can we get him to stay for dinner? Think of something!"

"I'm thinking, I'm thinking—" What he was thinking was more like how to get his mother out of there.

"Mooooom!" yelled Jeff. "Christopher's here."

Dale didn't know what they were having for dinner, but the house smelled like spaghetti or something Italian—smells that could twist anybody's arm.

"What's he doing here?" Meredith asked. She crossed the room, bracelets clinking, to where he waited at the front door.

"Christopher, are you out of your mind?" she yelled when she looked out. "You can't make social calls in Detweiler's finest."

He grinned. "Not to worry, it's perfectly legit.

Somebody has to do the chores. Here." He handed her the flowers. "I remembered you were having a dinner party, so I brought you a centerpiece."

At that point Meredith had to laugh. "Are these from the ten-o'clock or the two-o'clock service? And how come you're so cheap?"

"They're yesterday's," he said, "so you better water 'em."

"Cathy"—she swung around—"I want you to meet a colleague. This is Christopher, the unstable one I've been telling you about."

Dale's mom smiled and put out her hand.

"Oh dear," Christopher muttered, "if there's anything I hate, it's offering an icy-cold hand to a beautiful woman." He did anyway. "My apologies, but I've just been through the car wash with that baby."

"This is Dale, Cathy's son," Meredith went on. "Her daughter Lindsey's in the family room doing homework. Like a good gymnast."

Dale nodded, hoping he wouldn't have to shake hands.

Jeff kind of stood there and grinned, his eyebrows acknowledging the fact that Christopher and Dale's mom looked pretty good together—her being short, him being medium and with good shoulders. Ages were hard for Dale, but Christopher's wind-mussed hair was thinning on top, a sign he'd been around awhile.

Ten minutes later all six of them were sitting at Meredith's dining-room table. Dale didn't have a clue as to who asked Christopher to stay, but there he was, filling his plate with manicotti and making everyone laugh about the fun of being head coachman at Detweiler's Funeral Home.

"I was so glad to get out of there today," he said. "It gets so I can't stand that sad organ music. Same thing—all day, all night. Coming up here, I tuned into KRC-Rock on the coach stereo. What a relief!"

Meredith rolled her eyes. "He's a disgrace to the profession, Cathy. I pretend I don't know him."

"Actually," he said, handing the salad bowl to Dale, "all I could think about today was the marinara sauce you described before pathology. I knew I had to have some."

He turned to speak to Lindsey. "She was talking about this recipe with the mushrooms, see? And how she'd simmer the sauce all day long? Oh, my gastrics!" He clutched his stomach.

Lindsey giggled. Christopher looked at Dale's mom next, who was across the table. "Do you have any idea how we interns eat? And *where* we eat when we're on call?"

She laughed as if she could guess, but the picture Dale was getting sort of turned his stomach.

"You just wait, Meredith." Christopher nodded. "You become a trainee this summer, right? Your

119

turn's coming. You get to live over there with the bodies."

"If I get through chemistry. And restorative art. Honestly, Christopher, did you see how pale I made that woman last week? I just hate using that power sprayer. I can't get the hang of it."

Jeff made a sprayer sound that got Dale laughing so hard he sprayed salad all over his plate.

Christopher didn't act as if he noticed. He just shrugged and went on talking shop with Meredith. "*Pale* is something people expect. You hear what happened with Bob Smedley's first case? He's color-blind, you know, a terrible handicap in this business. You might get by with a high blush, but making someone bright red? With bright-red hands? We put this tasteful little sign on his door that said, 'Better Bodies by Bob.' "

Meredith choked. Dale cracked up, too, but he couldn't believe how his mom was flipping out with the rest of them. Laughing about dead people was gross, wasn't it? He wondered why she found everything Christopher said so funny.

"You guys tell me if you hate hearing me talk like this." Christopher looked at Dale's mom, but was reading *Dale's* mind. "Some people would think I'm being disrespectful."

Dale didn't know what to think exactly. Christopher was funny as anything, but it didn't seem right to be talking the way he was. Jeff just went on stuffing his face, so Dale guessed he was used to it, living with Meredith.

A little later, when they got on the subject of how some people wanted to be buried—with their cats or their favorite running shoes—Dale got up enough courage to blurt out, "I'd rather be cremated any day."

"Dale!" came his mother, as if he'd said something wrong.

"Way to go, kid." Christopher shook his head. "Put me out of business!"

They all stopped talking for a while to eat, but Dale felt hot and kind of prickly. He hoped someone would change the subject.

When Meredith got up for more garlic bread, she said, "This guy's not your ordinary funeral-director type, Cathy, but he keeps all of us in that college saner than we would be otherwise."

"You deal with death day after day," Christopher said, suddenly serious, "and after a while you tell yourself, 'Come on, you got to lighten up.' A kid who's been hit on a bike comes in in a bag, you know? A death like that gets to you. I know making jokes sounds sick, but it's how I cope."

What Christopher was saying made sense to Dale, but he still wasn't sure he liked him much. He hoped his mom wasn't liking him too much, either, though she seemed to be hanging on his every word.

Before they left Jeff's house that night, Christopher had asked Dale's mom to the new planetarium show being advertised. What was worse, she'd accepted. Dale couldn't believe it. The whole idea made him shudder.

"Will you stop being such a sourpuss, Dale?" she scolded him later in the car.

"You don't even know him!" he pointed out, as if that were the problem.

"So? I'll get to know him. He makes me laugh. Believe me, I need a laugh now and then. And he might like a home-cooked meal occasionally. Did you hear how he has to scrounge to stay in school?"

Oh no! Already she'd made him into a *cause.* What was wrong with John if she wanted to cook for someone? John would like a good home-cooked meal, he bet. His daughter looked like the type who'd need a recipe to boil water.

Dale scooted down in his seat and energetically crossed his arms over his chest. Maybe Chris the Cut-Up would arrive in his biggest, blackest hearse next Saturday and she'd refuse to get in. He himself wouldn't be caught dead riding in a funeral coach, no matter what stupid color it was.

"Well, I think he's cute!" Lindsey piped up from the backseat. "He told me he was a gymnast once himself, but he was never very good." She burbled on. "He also said he was a cowboy one summer. In Wyoming."

"That computes," Dale muttered.

"Maaaaammas, don't let your babies grow up to be cowboys," sang his mom, half laughing, as she pulled into their driveway and parked. Now she was teasing *him*.

Dale figured nothing he said would make any difference. He might as well save his breath.

The evening didn't quite end there. His mom sent Lindsey in so she could get to bed, but she kept him in the car.

"I have to pick up Matt over at Jamie's," she said, "but I want you to listen to me a minute." She twisted around to face him. "We have to go on in this family. We can't stop living our lives. Your dad wouldn't want us to."

"I know."

"It's been hard, hasn't it? And this winter—oh, wow! It's really been the pits. Especially for you because you take all our problems on yourself."

"How come I do that?"

"You're like your dad. You're just like David." She reached over and smoothed his hair. "That's one reason I love you so much. But I want you to know we'll be all right. I'm the mom and I'll keep us going. Can you trust me to do that?"

He nodded, glad it was dark so she couldn't see the lie in his eyes.

She turned around and put the gearshift on *R*. "So

get your butt to bed and stop worrying. I'll be home in a minute."

Dale watched her back down the driveway, then slowly walked up to the house. Maybe he *was* getting to be an old sourpuss. Why couldn't he just lighten up and let his mom do the worrying, like she said? He knew why. He wasn't convinced. He didn't believe she could keep them going without someone else's help. If she didn't find somebody soon, someone solid like John, the responsibility for their family would fall on him. And that was the scariest part.

Wearily, Dale climbed the steps to his room. She was right about one thing—winter had definitely been the pits. Now, with crazy Christopher in the picture, he didn't know what to expect.

chapter 13

"This is not one of my better trades," Dale said, watching Jeff count out change for a new spiral notebook.

"I wouldn't pay up except I'm sick of you taking all my paper," Jeff muttered.

They'd met early at the middle-school bookstore so Jeff could make good on his bet. The night before, when challenged, Dale had done a perfect "360° boneless," though he'd broken a kingpin on his skateboard in the process.

In the hall again, Dale backed Jeff into a garbage can where he gave him the rattling he deserved. He had to act mad, of course, but getting a free notebook was okay by him.

Especially today. Friday. Essay day in the Okimoto Armory.

Rumor had it that three seventh graders had wiped out of English boot camp since September. No way did *he* want to be barracks'd in a class where he could make A's and B's.

"Thanks," Dale remembered to say by the time they reached the water cooler. "If you weren't such a good friend I'd beat you bloody."

Jeff gave a laugh. "You and how many platoons? Hey, you want to cruise awhile?"

"Not really."

"We got fifteen minutes. What do you want to do?"

"I don't know." Dale's mind was still back at the bookstore, wondering if they could use a student clerk. There had to be some way to earn money besides delivering papers. If he had a decent bike, he could make enough to buy a bike. Classic catch-22.

Still frowning, Dale jiggled a combination lock and waited for Jeff to get a drink.

"Something I can't figure," he said, "is why your mom and that Christopher guy want to be in the funeral business. You couldn't pay me—"

"It's one of the safer lines of work," Jeff chuckled as they started up again.

"What do you mean, safe? Who says? What if you fell in a grave and broke your leg? And nobody found you. And there came a big flood—"

"I didn't say *grave digging* was safe, dummy. My mom's not studying to be a gravedigger—what do you think? But listen, I read these figures in one of mom's trade magazines. Did you know it's as dangerous to be a garbage collector as to be a cop?"

Dale gave him a skeptical look, but Jeff went on. "Yeah, and being an athlete is no more dangerous than being a pharmacist. Or a stockbroker."

Just then Lizette and her friends, heading the other way, passed in a cloud of perfume.

Dale's eyes sought Lizette's. There! What was it? A millionth of a second's worth of eye contact? It was enough. As one man, Jeff and Dale swung around and headed back in the direction of the bookstore.

Lesson from mom's notebook, the page on Christopher: Don't pass up a chance, no matter how unlikely.

The announcement they'd all been waiting for came at the beginning of first period when Mrs. Delacruz, the principal, got on the intercom.

"Seventh graders, your attention, please," she said in a firm voice. "There will be notices going to your homes next week about the maturation program, Understanding Our Bodies. We hope every student will be in attendance with his or her parent, Wednesday night, April twelfth. Put it on your calendars."

Someone whispered loudly, "Is that the sex talk?"

On mention of the *S* word, there was a general embarrassed snickering, with Mrs. Okimoto the only one in the room with a perfectly straight face.

There was more: "I'm going to depend on you excellent students to approach this educational emphasis with maturity and respect."

The "maturity and respect" also caused a ripple.

"Have a good day now," she finished. "And remember, *trash belongs in the containers*. Only five students wore the Ima Pig and Neanderthal buttons yesterday, so we're getting better. Keep up the good work."

At the end of announcements Mrs. Okimoto slid up onto her desk, still marking roll, and waited for the general buzz to subside.

"Is there anyone here who doesn't know what we mean by AIDS?" she asked.

No one raised a hand. You'd have to be in the Australian Outback not to know about AIDS, Dale figured, and he was pretty sure word had leaked in even there.

"So! I guess we won't write about that."

The room was so quiet Dale could hear himself inhale, exhale, inhale.

Finally, Okimoto cracked a smile. "Have I ever asked you to write on the subject of what makes the world go 'round?"

"No," someone answered.

"Do you know what that expression refers to?"

They didn't, or pretended not to. Dale had an idea.

"Love," she said. "Love makes the world go 'round. It's from an old song, based on eons of observation." She twisted around, laid the roll book on her desk. "I suppose it's true—taken loosely and figuratively."

Dale studied the back of Lizette's head and wondered what she was thinking. If their teacher made them go into "buzz boxes" to talk about love, he, for one, would die.

"In April," Okimoto continued, "you'll be learning some very important things about yourselves and your relationships with the opposite sex, but much of what you learn will be vocabulary and data. What I call 'technical stuff.' Of course, everyone needs information, at whatever age.

"In this class, I prefer to concentrate on the more idealistic aspects. It's my opinion that love is as legitimate a topic for us to discuss as sex. Sometimes, with the dangers of disease being so terrifying, we tend to forget about the love part, don't we?"

Dale straightened and looked around. Every kid

in the room had run up antennas to better catch her words.

After more talk about how love makes people behave and about different kinds of love, she handed out a sheet with ten topics to choose from and said they were to write an essay. She wanted to see their clustering efforts, a good topic sentence, and some sort of outline by the end of the period.

"Remember how we sometimes cluster our ideas on the board? Same thing. Avoid generalizations, be specific. And as always, only honest writing counts in this class, so no faking." She glanced at the clock. "Thirty minutes, so you'll have to hustle."

Dale spent the first five trying to decide whether he'd write one called "My Ideal Girl" or "The Kind of Parent I'd Like to Be." Maybe, he thought with a grin, he'd just sabotage the assignment and do "My Ideal Guy," a topic intended for the girls. Hey, he could do this character sketch of a first baseman he admired a lot!

No, he'd better not. She'd kill him. He squirmed a bit more, knowing every male in the class who wrote about his ideal girl would be describing Lizette. Imagine getting a dozen essays on Lizette. Sickening. So maybe he'd write about what kind of parent he'd like to be when he grew up. That sounded easier, anyway.

Dale opened his new notebook, tore out a

sheet, wrote the first thing that came to mind: "I want to be the kind of dad who does things with his kids."

He stared out the window a minute, thinking of the great times he'd had growing up. Had his father had as much fun with him as he'd always *seemed* to be having? He wondered about that a lot, now that he was older himself.

He looked down, wrote, "If my son wants to check out *Pirate Jim* from the library 85 times and wants me to read it to him that many, I will."

Every Saturday, for most of a year . . . fish and chips, a candy bar from Smith's . . . a trip to the library . . . reading Pirate Jim *together in the big black rocker . . .*

The ideas came in a stream after that, almost too fast to get them down. "I'll play video games, won't cheat to make kids feel good, won't say I'm too busy. Explain stuff—" Breaking down the explaining, he wrote "hard math, advrbs, why Gran. Shrwd is afraid to ride in a plane, elctricty—" Abbreviations flew from his fingers, to heck with spelling.

"Down on the floor—crazy—get silly—red in the face. Let my kid beat the tar out of me once," he wrote, grinning to remember, "so he'll know how good it feels to be big."

Dale swung around to check the clock. Only eighteen minutes? He wiped his sweaty hands on his jeans. He'd never get everything down. There was too much. It was like assembling a hundred-piece puzzle against a stopwatch.

As he read over his notes, it suddenly occurred to him what he was doing. He was writing about his dad, not himself. *That* wasn't the assignment. Dale frowned at the paper. He wasn't trying to write about his dad; it just came out that way. Would it be fair, describing your own father? Could you call that honest writing?

He poked a hole in the paper, then another.

Finally he crumpled it up. He'd do his essay on "My Ideal Girl."

Quickly he opened his notebook and began again.

"My ideal girl," he wrote for starters, "is beautiful."

He smiled blissfully. Why not stop there? That said it all, didn't it? Who didn't want a beautiful girl or a great-looking guy?

Cliché! He could see Okimoto's favorite word scrawled across the top of his paper in red.

Okay, so much for beautiful.

Dale chewed his pencil and gazed at Lizette's bent head and the way she hunched over her paper. If only he could figure out what it was that everybody liked about her, he'd have the key. Teachers and girls liked her as well as guys, so there had to be reasons. Other than her hair . . . and the curvy arms that drove Jeff wild . . .

Then, exactly like in the cartoons, a light popped on. What he wrote next was "My ideal girl is beautiful to be with." He took a deep breath. Right, now he was on the track. Three little words. How could they make so much difference?

"She talks about interesting things," he added. "She listens. She laughs a lot and makes me feel good. She's kind."

Dale's gaze returned to the window. If he was being really down-to-the-inch honest, his ideal girl would like to eat and would know how to cook. She'd like sports, too, because in their family eating and sports usually went together.

Quickly, he made two columns, labeled one side "food she likes" and the other, "sports."

On the left he listed candy, popcorn, peanut butter cookies, root beer shakes, taco salad, nachos, pork chops and applesauce. Okimoto had asked for specifics, hadn't she? On the sports side, he had to stop and think. He didn't know what sports Lizette liked. But he was supposed to be making this up, wasn't he? He started with softball, feeling pretty sure her favorites would be the same as his. She had told Carol once, in his presence, that she was dying to try waterskiing sometime.

Under the word *appearance* he put "nice clothes, shiny skin, clean, but not afraid to get dirty." Another heading brought out "not a big spender on dates—studies the menu board, orders cheap. Likes to hug and kiss on certain occasions, hold hands in the movies."

Dale stopped writing. He glanced up to locate Mrs. Okimoto. How would he know if he liked that stuff or not? He'd never kissed anyone but his mom and Grandma Sherwood when he had to. He erased the mushy part, not sure if he was being honest or dishonest, but hurrying to get rid of it.

He craned to check the time again. Four minutes! A disaster. He'd never make it. Blowing a strand of hair out of his eyes, he slouched down in his seat to see what he had so far.

It wasn't until he read the word *menu*—and thought of Wendy's—that he began to realize what he'd done. With his first try he'd described his dad. Everything on *this* page—every blasted thing!—fit his mom to a tee. What was he, some kind of weirdo? He wasn't in love with his mom! But the person he'd just described was exactly like his mom. Right down to the taco salad, for crying out loud! If he'd mentioned country music, his ideal girl would be a clone.

Mrs. Okimoto, apparently seeing him crumple up the second sheet, walked back to his desk and asked what was wrong.

All he could do was shrug. He couldn't tell *her*. She guessed. "I'm rushing you too much, right?"

"Yeah," he said in an injured tone of voice, "you are."

"Class," she interrupted them, "if planning drafts are ready for checking off this hour, fine. If not, I'll collect all finished essays Monday. Your writing is important to me. I can wait."

"Thanks," Dale said, though he didn't think she heard.

Saturday night was the real switcheroo. It was Dale who sat home watching the clock, waiting for his mom to come home from her date. Dishes were done, Lindsey and Matt were asleep, his papers (both of them) were written and waiting for him to choose which he'd hand in. By ten thirty he was looking out the front window for headlights.

Christopher had come out from the city on a bus, of all things. He'd arrived puffing and blowing from the walk up their hill, apologizing for his VW bug that needed engine work or an autopsy, he wasn't sure.

"I'll buy the gas if we can take your car," he'd said, very upfront. And though his mom hadn't exactly looked amused, they'd taken off for the planetarium in the old station wagon.

At least he hadn't arrived in "Detweiler's finest" this time. When Jeff had called that night to see, they'd had a good laugh over the fact that he was wearing the same thing as last Saturday, only with a flower in his coat pocket. Dale's mom had spent hours doing her eyes, which seemed a great waste if you were going out with someone who wore Levi's and a white flower at the same time.

At exactly 11:08 the garage door shook the house and Dale rushed out to meet his mom.

"Are you still up?" she said, grabbing him for a hug.

"I wasn't sleepy."

"Well, you're nice, but you didn't need to wait up."

They walked through the side door and into the kitchen together.

"Did you have fun?" Dale asked.

She kicked off her shoes. "Fun? I guess you could say that. Yes, after a fashion . . . fun." She opened the refrigerator. "Are you as hungry as I am?"

He was *always* hungry.

"Didn't you eat something with Christopher?" he asked.

"Are you kidding?" She took out milk, a package of hamburger, pickle relish, and ketchup. "How about a burger and some hot chocolate? Sound good?"

"Yeah! I'll fix the chips." He opened the cupboard and got out plates. "So what'd you guys do afterward?"

"You're not going to believe this, but he took me over to Detweiler's Funeral Home to show me 'his place.'"

"Mom!" Dale whirled around. "He took you to Casket City?"

"Detweiler's, Dale, please." She rolled up her sleeves and smacked out two hamburger patties on the cutting board. "Christopher did treat me to a Diet Coke out of the vending machine. As a matter of fact, we split one. Two paper cups, one Coke."

Dale shook his head in disbelief. "Cheap, huh, like Meredith says?"

"Well, broke, at least. After he bought gas for that monster car of ours, I had to chip in on tickets." She grinned across the counter at Dale.

"Wasn't it kind of creepy being in a funeral home . . . you know, at night?"

"A little." Suddenly she started laughing, and really hard.

"What?" Dale asked. "What's so funny?"

"You want to hear this? But only if you promise not to tell everyone—"

She salted and peppered the burgers, then walked over to sit by him.

"Christopher took me on this tour of the casket room that was absolutely hilarious. I can't wait to tell Meredith."

"Mom! You went in the casket room?"

"Now listen. First he put on this tape, 'Yellow Submarine.' You know it? It's a great old Beatles number. So *that* was blasting out of the speakers the whole time we were in there. Then he said he could tell a lot about a woman by the kind of casket she'd pick out for herself.

"I mean, Dale, what a line! He goes, 'What do you prefer on interiors, this nice blue crepe or a pale crushed velvet?' Then he asked if I'd care to test drive one of the display models."

"Test drive!" Dale squeaked. "That guy's nuts."

"He is!" she went on, her eyes dancing and her hands going. "But those embalming students have these code names for every casket. One's a Chevy, another's an MG. They talk about racing stripes, of all things. Christopher showed me this thick, solid-bronze number. That was a Rolls, I think . . . and next to it was a cherry hardwood. Very popular, very 'in,' he said, like he was really trying to move those cars off the lot."

"So did you pick one out?" Dale asked, pointing to the burgers to remind her, but fascinated by what she was saying.

"What do you think? About halfway through the tour, Christopher gave me this long, analytical look and asked if I'd ever thought of parting my hair on the other side. That guy just can't stop being a mortician, even on a date. No, Dale, I just laughed and walked out. I told him I never buy anything that isn't on sale."

"Hmmmmm. Do you like him a little?" Dale ventured.

"Of course, he's very likable." She stirred chocolate into their cups. "But, you know, I'm thirty-seven. I have three kids, one who's hardly cost-effective"—her glance rose to the cupboards—"and a hefty mortgage on this house. I don't want to repeat my struggling student days."

Dale nodded and listened. He wouldn't tell her how relieved he was that Christopher hadn't moved ahead of John on the charts.

She added relish and ketchup to the great-smelling hamburgers, then brought them to the counter and sat down.

"Hey," she said a minute later around a bite, "I'm getting this smashing idea. Wouldn't it be easier to have an imaginary boyfriend? You know, sort of like what Matt does? Only I wouldn't call him Waggy, of course."

Dale snorted into his cup. It was okay with him, what with Blake and the imaginary girlfriend he'd had ever since Friday.

"I love it! I really do," she said in a rush. "I could drag him home anytime I got lonesome, the way Matt does. Make him a sandwich like this. We'd sit and talk. I'd pretend he loved country."

139

Dale swung around. "Use your head, Mom. Make him a big recording star while you're at it. Why not?" If Matt could make round trips to the North Pole every day, his mom could have Randy Travis for a boyfriend.

She pulled a face. "With my luck, he'd turn out to be one of those . . . disenfranchised cowboys."

Dale switched to his soulful mode. " 'I'm just a country boy' "—hand on heart—" 'Money have I none—' "

His mom joined in: " 'But I've got silver in the stars, Gold in the morning sun.' " Touching heads, they dragged out another " 'Gold in the morning suuuuuuun.' " His mom's frantic eyes told him he was way off key. Dale grinned. He couldn't help it. He'd inherited his dad's musical *in*ability.

"Guess what," he said after another bite. "You have to put April twelfth on the calendar. The maturation thing's that night."

His mother sat up straight. "So soon?"

"And you don't need to go with me this time. I'll just go on over with Jeff and his dad."

"You mean it's going to be girls-to-the-cafeteria, boys-to-the-gym again? *Daddies only* with their sons?"

The hamburger suddenly went dry in his throat. "I think so."

"Dale, I hate that!" She smacked the counter with

both hands. "Why do they do this to all of us single parents? It's totally insensitive."

Dale couldn't think of an answer.

"I'm sorry, but this really bugs me. I'm not going to put up with being humiliated again this year, Dale, I'm just not."

She carried her plate to the sink and angrily scraped the remains of her sandwich into the garbage disposal. "And I'm not providing you with any father substitute, so forget that right now."

Dale jutted out his bottom lip, pretending to sulk.

"Waggy would have liked the end of your burger," he said to get her happy again.

As it turned out, Dale spent an hour Sunday writing a completely new essay. How in the world had Mrs. Okimoto got three essays out of him when she'd only assigned one?

To the topic "What *Not* to Do on a Date" he'd added his own subtitle—"With an Undertaker." In his opinion, it was his funniest paper yet. When the undertaker said to his girlfriend, "Want to try this one on for size?" a nearby corpse sat straight up in the casket and sent her screaming.

chapter 14

The next weekend, Dale's mother couldn't get to the phone soon enough to talk things over with Meredith.

"Will Bob be taking Jeff?" she asked. "Dale's having a fit . . . oh, he's not?"

She turned from the phone to look at Dale, who was loading the dishwasher and listening. She covered the mouthpiece and whispered, "Bob has a Masonic thing that night."

Dale's heart sank. He'd almost convinced her to let him go with Jeff.

"Look, Meredith, if we're both stuck with this . . .

remember how awful it was last year? You're right, I went along, but I was wimpier then."

And weepier, Dale remembered. She'd gone to pieces after they got home—more from being mad than sad, he'd thought at the time.

She said, "What are you doing right now? Can you come over? I've made up my mind to protest— if I have to I'll do it alone, but I'd be braver with a friend."

"What's she going to protest?" asked Lindsey as she plopped her homework on the dining-room table.

"Ask *her*!" Dale snapped. Didn't his mom care about how mortified he'd be if she picketed or wrote letters or did any of the things she was threatening to do? Didn't she have enough trouble being the mother in this family without trying to be the father, too?

"Tell her I'm at Jeff's," Dale said as he pulled a sweatshirt on over his head. "I can't stand it."

He practically knocked Matt down charging out the door. When Matt asked for help getting his kite in the air, Dale yelled, "No, I'm going someplace, can't you see?"

Matt blinked fast and remained there on the porch, holding a yellow dragon kite that was bigger than he was. "Later, huh, when you come back?"

Dale didn't answer. He just took off on his bike.

Great going! he told himself, coasting down Peruvian to where Jeff lived. Some father you'll be, all patience and understanding. Shoot! What was his mom trying to do to him, anyway?

Word could get around school so fast. Just when he was making progress with Lizette, too. He was positive she'd been describing him in her Ideal Guy essay. Who else would she know who was tall, brown-haired, funny, besides being a good writer? She'd gone four shades of purple when Okimoto made them read each other's papers in critique groups.

"I like that guy myself," Dale had joked after reading hers. He thought she might give him a clue, but she just avoided his eyes and mumbled, "Thanks, but yours is the best. Nobody in class is ever as original as you are."

She'd think he was original, all right, when she heard how his mother crashed seventh-grade maturation and single-handedly slew three father dragons to get in the door.

Dale found Jeff cleaning winter trash off the grass, so he got another rake out of the garage and helped.

When Jeff's mom left, saying she'd be at Cathy's, she stopped beside Dale to say, "Your mom's really ticked off about this maturation business, isn't she?"

Dale nodded. "I may run away."

She laughed, made him turn around to see if he

was ready for another haircut. "I've thought of splitting a few times in my life, but not lately." She patted him on the shoulder. "Don't worry about it, you hear? And Jeff, if Christopher comes to study, send him up to get me."

Once she was gone, Jeff dropped onto the front steps and pulled Dale down by the band of his sweatshirt. "I just had a radical idea," he said with a look Dale recognized.

Dale grinned back. "Me, too."

"Christopher!" they shouted together. Of course they had to howl and slap hands and go through their rigamarole.

"So how do we get him to take us?" Jeff asked.

"Call him. Right now while she's gone. Later, you know, when things are cool, tell her we took the matter into our own hands. Your mom's not as big on doing this as mine, anyway."

They walked into the house, making cracks about the kind of father sub Christopher would make for the maturation program. Dale could just hear him when they hauled out the body charts. He knew more about bodies than any of their gym teachers.

After several tries at the phone, however, they gave up.

"I don't want to waste my whole life on this, do you?" Jeff said in disgust. "We'll figure something out."

"Okay, Ellis, but you had your dad last year. Remember how I ended up sitting with that guy whose son didn't show? It was like 'Here, have a foster dad,' and over there at the gym door, Mom was looking in like she'd just been robbed of her citizenship. I hated it!"

Jeff threw up his hands. "All right, all right! We'll work on it, but I thought we were going to check the want ads for jobs today. Jeez!" He grabbed up the Sunday paper.

"I already did. There's nothing."

"Here's one for a nanny," Jeff said. "Want to apply?"

"Might as well. I'm already a management-level baby-sitter."

"It's the time of year," Jeff said dismally. "Nothing happens between snow shoveling and lawn mowing."

In the end, they returned to the front steps, downed a couple of Cokes, and talked about girls.

The afternoon was half over when Dale pumped back up the hill and offered to put a tail on Matt's kite.

For the next two hours the uncertainties of his life evaporated. He was up there in the sky, a speck with a red flannel tail—dipping, circling, soaring ever higher on the currents. He *was* the kite!

When it tugged on the string like something alive and Matt screamed with delight, Dale realized he hadn't had so much fun in ages.

Who needed maturation? He didn't want to be mature *or* an adolescent. He just wanted to be a kid. Like Matt. A kid flying a kite.

chapter 15

The morning of April twelfth, Dale found his mother reading her horoscope in the *Gazette*. She was trying for last-minute advice before making her big move, no doubt. Meredith, Jeff told him, was so panicked she'd visited an astrologer and had herself charted.

"Don't bother figuring mine," Dale said sarcastically as he sat down and poured milk on his Cheerios. "It goes, 'This is a good day for dropping out. See a movie instead.' "

His mother didn't look up until she had her string of words down on paper. "You may hate me now," she said, nodding at him, "but one of these days you'll appreciate your mother."

"One of these days, hah! One of these days I won't be around. What's it say, anyway?"

She folded the newspaper and stood up. "Oh, Dale, I don't pay any attention. It's just for fun."

He wondered.

Matt showed up next, reminding everyone that the Scrabble game in the bottom of the Cheerios box was his. "Can I get it now, Mom? Please, can I?"

Dale handed him the box and watched him peer inside. It was against the rules at their house to dig for prizes, but waiting caused Matt unspeakable agony.

Lindsey arrived behind Matt. As usual, she began breakfast by giving her yogurt a noisy stirring, a ritual Dale hated.

"I have to baby-sit tonight, huh?" she said to anyone listening. "Because Dale has to go to his . . . ummm . . . special deal at school."

She threw him a needling glance.

Dale had a powerful urge to punch her out, but his mom was suddenly right there in his face, saying "NO!"

The day went downhill from there, in spite of having a magnificent fantasy all through math: Dale packing his bag, Dale hitchhiking, Dale getting a ride with a long-haired girl in a BMW, then saying good-bye at the state line, where she gave him a bundle of money and wished him well.

By the time they left the house that night, Dale was a wreck.

On millions of occasions he'd wished to have his dad back again, alive and well and head of their family. He didn't know if he'd ever wished it harder than right now.

Jeff, too, looked grim when he climbed into the backseat in his Sunday slacks, smelling like soap. After exchanging "hi's" they drove most of the way without talking.

"Did Christopher get you that press card?" Dale's mom said the one time she opened her mouth.

Meredith patted her purse. "It's right here. My last resort. I hope I don't have to use it, 'cause I sure don't have the right I.D."

Jeff raised his eyebrows, but Dale didn't have a clue as to what they were talking about. Actually, he didn't *want* to know what they were talking about. They might have guns in their purses for all he knew. *My mother the radical! Oh, man, how am I going to get through this?*

Kids were waiting all over the lobby, standing around looking at each other while their parents talked. Dale recognized their little neighborhood knot, but hoped his mom wouldn't join them. It wasn't at all like school for seventh graders to be so subdued and serious.

Jeff was the first to spot the big arrows that told them where to go.

"Where's the one that says 'Exit'?" he asked, making Dale laugh in spite of his misery.

The arrows pointed opposite directions—one instructing "Fathers and Sons to the Boys' Gym," and the other "Mothers and Daughters to the Cafeteria."

Dale's mother stopped, took a deep breath, said to Meredith, "Well, here goes nothin'. We might as well be on time."

Dale kept his eyes straight ahead as he marched along next to Jeff. He was glad the locker hall that led to the gym was semidark, but he wished the school weren't so quiet. Their moms' heels made sharp noises that definitely sounded out of place.

They followed other boys and their fathers right up to the gym door, where they could see in. Dale could feel his heart hammering inside his chest. Aside from the principal, there wasn't another woman in sight.

Sure enough, Mr. Bauer, one of the teachers, caught them before they'd gone six steps into the gym.

"We'd rather have the boys alone if they don't have dads with them," he said with a smile Dale knew would infuriate his mom.

She didn't flinch, however. She just stood there and looked at Mr. Bauer as if he'd taken leave of his senses. "Oh, but Dale is my son. I'm a single parent now. I'm the responsible adult in our family."

Dale shrank to half his original size, but Mr. Bauer wasn't about to be challenged.

"Boys," he said, "would you show your mothers to the library so they won't get lost? We have a special program planned for you who had to drive your youngsters over but wouldn't be attending."

"Excuse me," Dale's mother said, and taking his hand as if he were two instead of thirteen, she walked him right past Mr. Bauer and on into the gym.

Dale looked back. Jeff threw him a baffled look, as if he'd somehow been picked for the wrong team. Meredith, still standing there, was into her purse digging for something. Tear gas? A stun gun? Dale was so nervous he'd just stopped thinking straight.

It was Mrs. Delacruz herself who hurried over to confront them next. Smiling nice as pie, she maneuvered his mom around and headed her back toward the door. Dale trailed behind like an afterthought.

"I'm sorry," she said firmly, "you wouldn't feel a bit welcome here. Separating our students like this makes sense. It's traditional for a good reason: We want the boys to feel free to ask questions."

Who was she kidding? Nobody ever asked questions.

"I'm the principal here," she went on, still smiling

big, "and I suspect you're Mrs. Purcell."

Abruptly, his mom stopped and pulled her arm away. "You did receive my letters, then, which nobody bothered to answer."

"The secretary made several calls, but she never found you at home."

"That's right. I work. But I would assume the school still uses the postal service?"

Dale couldn't believe what happened next. Mr. Bauer was approaching them, *escorting* Meredith into the gym. Jeff's face was pink going on fuchsia, but he kept up with his mom, the sound of his Reeboks magnified as things grew quiet and people began seeing what was happening.

"She has a press card—" Mr. Bauer said out of the side of his mouth as he swept by, "I can't keep her out unless you want us featured in the news."

"Oh, don't tell me!" Mrs. Delacruz was finally starting to sound as cross as Dale figured she was.

Glancing at the boys and dads already seated— longing to sprint *anywhere*—Dale saw guys he knew, many since grade school. Some smiled, waved. He turned his back, wanting to die.

Simultaneously, Mrs. Okimoto herself walked into the gym with her son, Kevin. The two of them sauntered along as casually as if it were a basketball game they were attending. They didn't get far, either.

The vice principal met them, his arms out like a barricade. Although he was twice her size, Dale had the feeling he'd just met his match. In her students' eyes, at least, Okimoto was unstoppable.

Mrs. Delacruz, still wanting to have her way, coaxed everybody over to one side, saying "Let's move and let these other people in." She then went into a spiel about their ten-year precedent and the kind of civic-minded attitudes that support school policies. "We've had great success doing it this way in the past," she kept saying. On and on.

Kevin gave Dale a shy grin. They'd never had any classes together, but suddenly they were brothers. "Today the gym—" Dale said like the terrified revolutionary he'd become, "tomorrow the locker room!"

Kevin laughed. So did Dale, finally.

Mrs. Okimoto then began laying out her case, but Mrs. Delacruz was plainly in no mood to listen to one of her own teachers.

"All right!" Dale's mom broke in with one of her "this is final" gestures. Dale sucked in his breath. Was she about to give in? With scared, pasty-faced Meredith already installed on the bleachers, was his own mom going to cave in? Suddenly he didn't want her to. He couldn't feel any worse than he already did. And it *was* unjust, the school's outdated policy. If he took himself out of the picture, he could see it.

He watched his mother's chin go up. When she spoke it was with frightening calm. "I'm going to accompany my son and remain in this gymnasium for the maturation program. If you don't allow me to stay, I'll bring suit against the school under the equal protection clause of the Constitution."

Suddenly Dale felt like cheering. His mother wasn't a crack legal secretary for nothing!

"My rights as a single parent are at issue here"— she looked Mrs. Delacruz straight in the eye—"and I'll take whatever legal remedies are necessary to redress what I consider a wrong. I don't plan to leave."

"That makes two of us!" said Mrs. Okimoto, loud enough for the bodyguards to hear.

Dale was only faintly aware of someone testing the mike as they took their seats on the top row of bleachers, dead center. Never, in his wildest dreams, had he pictured himself watching the seventh-grade maturation movies with his English teacher. The two mothers, talking excitedly, seemed thrilled to have had each other for backup.

A minute later, Kevin hauled gum out of his pocket and gave Dale a stick. "I'm used to being different," he said with a shrug.

Dale grinned and thanked him. They were different, all right. It was like he'd said to Jeff, his mom wasn't the same person she'd been three years ago. Tonight she was one tough mother! Maybe she didn't need his help, after all. Or Richard's. Or even John's. One thing he knew for sure. His dad would be giving her the "thumbs up" if he could see her now.

chapter 16

The school bus rattled so loud going over chuck-holes it was hard to have a conversation. Every spring, the same thing. Someday, Dale figured, an entire busload of kids would disappear in one of the craters.

Sitting beside Jeff and staring off, Dale counted only four more Mondays before vacation. To think he could call himself an eighth grader come summer. He'd find a job. He'd save up for a mountain bike, buy some clothes with labels, give the rest of the money to his mom. He'd also ask Lizette to a movie if he could get up his nerve.

Amazingly, she was still speaking to him.

Amazingly, so was everyone else.

Mostly because Mrs. Okimoto insisted they have a discussion *after* maturation night. That's when the kids asked questions. Good ones, too, knowing she'd tell them the truth. They also talked about the "mini protest," as Okimoto was calling it, with its maxi results. Next year, rumor had it, their sex education would be co-ed and a regular part of health classes.

Now, nearing home with three daylight hours ahead, Dale realized Jeff still hadn't spent one nickel of his allowance.

"If we bike down to Smith's we could maybe find a good video," he said. They hadn't seen *Ooze* or *Teenage Scumbag*, a new release.

Jeff, his head resting on the seat back, answered, "Okay by me, but I get to pick. Let's see if *Ooze* is in."

Dale hid his grin. "You always get to pick."

"You pay, you pick, dummy. That's life."

Dale himself couldn't imagine getting five dollars a week to spend as he pleased. Every Saturday, like clockwork, Mr. Ellis stopped by Jeff's to deliver the allowance in person.

"Mostly to check on Mom," Jeff told him once when they were talking serious, "to see if she's keeping things up. I also think he gets lonesome."

"Meet me in ten," Jeff said as they slapped hands and he swung off the bus at his corner.

In less time than that they were coasting down Peruvian on their bikes.

Without a single hint from Dale, Jeff shelled out for two Snickers bars as soon as they got in the store. Someday, Dale pledged in a spasm of gratitude, he was going to do something extra nice for Jeff.

As always, they cruised back to the produce section to see if Mr. Ellis was working—which he was—and to say "hi."

"Be your mamma comin' down to croon?" he said right off to Dale.

Dale didn't have the slightest idea which accent Jeff's dad was using or what he was talking about.

"What do you mean?" asked Jeff.

"Big doin's. It's Single Shoppers' Night again Wednesday." Mr. Ellis tied on a clean apron. "They're importing a group. Country, bluegrass . . . Cathy's kind, anyway. Singing competition and big prizes. Smith's is making money off its singles, they can afford it."

"Hey, man!" Jeff swung around. "Your mom could win something, she's so good."

Dale ran a hand over the cool eggplants, his eyes narrowing. Jeff was right, she could win. Or she'd come close. That's how she'd paid her way through college, singing with a country band.

"You didn't see the sign?" Mr. Ellis asked. "You walked right by it."

Dale grabbed Jeff's collar and headed him back the way they'd come.

Sure enough, a huge painted announcement was right there next to the week's price busters.

Wednesday, 10 PM
The Down Under Gopher Band
COUNTRY WESTERN COMPETITION
You may not be Dolly, Reba, or Lynn—
But Singles, here's your chance to break in!
First Prize: $500
(Groceries or Cash)
Second Prize: $250
Third Prize: 10 large hand-thrown pizzas
Tickets to Highway 101 in Concert

"Gol, Dale"—Jeff hit him on the shoulder—"she has to enter."

"Five hundred bucks!" Dale sent up a prayer. "I could buy that amber yellow Ascent we saw. Great for hills. Eighteen speeds, cantilever brakes—"

"Come on, get real. The money would go for Lindsey's gymnastics. But I bet she'd win. I mean, even Richard said she sang like a pro, didn't he? I mean, even the pizza's *something*."

"Listen, Jeff, what I'm thinking is . . . if I had that

bike I could get a paper route. Mom's always saying it takes money to make money.''

"So you have to get her here first. She hates the idea, so how you gonna do it?"

Dale finished his candy bar, pocketed the wrapping, pulled out and straddled his pitifully inadequate BMX.

"Let's go to your place," he called as he shoved off. "We'll think of something, but I want a foolproof plan this time. I mean, totally foolproof. No stupid gum on the phone, okay?"

"Gum on the phone?" Jeff yelled as they pumped across the parking lot. "Who put the ad in wrong? That C. person who liked country music could have been Christopher or Clementine or Cuckoohead—"

"Yeah, yeah, so who's perfect?"

Halfway to Jeff's, Dale remembered why they'd gone to Smith's in the first place, but he didn't care. If he was as original as Lizette said he was, he'd get his mom to the singles' shindig. And if she was as gutsy as she'd been at the boys' gym, he had a hunch she'd sing.

Jeez, if it meant five hundred bucks *he*'d sing!

At exactly nine twenty Wednesday night, Dale was finishing a snack of peanut butter toast in his pajamas.

"You feel all right?" his mom asked as he started

up the stairs half an hour earlier than usual.

"Just tired. Maybe I'm getting something."

"Need an aspirin?"

"Nah, I'm okay."

"Well, keep your music off," she said, going back to her book. "Matt just fell asleep and Lindsey's studying."

Upstairs, he closed the door of his room and wiped both palms on his pajamas. She'd bought it! Now all he had to do was wait thirty minutes.

Lindsey, whose light was still showing under her door, was holding up her end of the deal, though it had cost him an I.O.U.

Dale moved the clock so he could see it better, then stretched out on his bed and closed his eyes.

Lizette appeared instantly—his proven best fantasy. Talking with her in his head, he was never tongue-tied, never embarrassed. He'd make up what she'd say to him, what he'd say back. Sometimes the brilliance of their conversations scared him, that was all.

When the clock said 10:03—odd numbers for luck!—he leaped out of bed with a little extra noise and went tearing down the stairs.

His mom looked up in alarm. "Are you sick?"

"Nooooo! I just remembered what I was supposed to do." He grabbed his head and flopped into a chair. "I forget everything. She'll kill me. And she gave me the easiest of anybody."

"What are you talking about?"

"Okimoto! We're having a party in class. Collectively, we wrote over fifty thousand words since September and so we're celebrating." He hoped she wouldn't get out her calculator, having snatched that figure out of the air. "I have to take potato chips tomorrow, and I forgot all about it."

"Oh, Dale!" Her shoulders sagged. "And we don't have a thing on hand. You kids finished the chips last night."

"Yeah, I know." Dale and Lindsey had made sure. "Do you have some change? I'll get dressed and go down on my bike."

She closed her book. "I can't believe those teachers! They think we're made of money or something?"

"She gave me the easiest, Mom. She knows you work. Some of the kids are taking salads, wieners. I wanted dip, but Jeff beat me to it." He stood up wearing his longest face. "Should I just say we can't afford it?"

"No, and you can't ride down there this time of night. I'll have to go myself. Hot dogs in English class! Anyone for education, I ask?"

"Wait a minute and I'll go with you. The kids like a certain kind."

"Oh, good grief! So hurry up. I don't want to be running around all night." She bent down to put on her shoes. "Tell Lindsey we're going, would you?"

163

Dale was grinning big, but his hands shook so hard he had a bad time buttoning his Levi's. He should win the Academy Award for what he'd just pulled off. If only everything else went as well.

"Don't rush," he heard Lindsey call down over the banister. "I'll be up an hour yet on this book report." Then she sneaked into his room, hunching her shoulders and laughing into her hands.

His mother was at the bottom of the steps, in the same jeans and oversized red shirt she'd been wearing. Not so hot, the sloppy look. There'd be single guys shopping, too. There was *that* to think of.

"Why don't you wear your silver belt?" he said on impulse. "Dad and I picked that one out for you and you never wear it."

Her mouth fell. "Whaaaaat?"

"I'll get it." He didn't give her a chance to object, just charged back to her room, lifted it off the hook, brought it out.

She had to laugh. "So it starts already? My Dale is getting clothes conscious? Only for his mother, not himself. You sure your socks match?"

She handed him her purse, buckled the silver medallion belt, then cuffed him one. "In two minutes I'll be out of the mood, so let's go."

Dale could hear the throbbing of the music as soon as they entered the parking lot. The place was so jammed they had to leave the car near the street edge, which gave Dale more time to get nervous than he wanted.

Only one other store was lighted, plus the fish-'n'-chips shop. The group was just ending "Somewhere Tonight."

"What's going on?" his mom asked. "Listen!" She stopped him. "Dale, that's a great steel guitar."

"What's the difference between a steel guitar and a plain one?" he asked, hoping she wouldn't guess about the singles part. Memories of Wendy's were suddenly strong and clear.

"Between steel and acoustic? The sound, for one thing. A steel guitar can wail. I better get oranges and milk while we're here. I swear, Dale, that music's live! Is it coming from Smith's?"

"Sounds like it."

Supposedly Jeff was inside buying dip if he hadn't screwed things up. Not that kids were invited to Singles' Night, but Jeff's dad said business was business and that they hadn't thrown anyone out yet. "No matter how young or married," was the way he'd put it.

Dale crossed his fingers and made a fierce wish. Somehow, he walked his mom past the sign on the window without her seeing it.

Once inside under fluorescent lights, it was clear that something was going on at their quiet neighborhood co-op. People were crammed in everywhere—standing and talking, trying to push through the aisles with their carts. Everyone seemed to be in a jolly mood. Where the buy-in-bulk barrels had been, four musicians were set up on a makeshift platform. A hand-clapping crowd had gathered around and people's shoulders were going.

"Hey, fun," his mother said, her face lighting up at once.

The guy with the bass guitar was now pumping out a good beat for "All My Exes Live in Texas." The drummer, young and red-haired, with the bluest eyes Dale had ever seen, was bouncing on his stool. Two more guys filled out the group, the bearded one strumming exactly like Dwight Yoakam. They were the real thing as far as Dale could tell: Levi's, boots, cowhide vests. Real scuffs on the boots.

When they slipped into "Lady Down on Love" for a change of tempo, Dale's mother melted. He wouldn't have believed such a meltdown if he hadn't been standing right there seeing it with his own eyes.

"Go find your potato chips," she said quietly. "I'll wait here."

He hadn't gone ten steps when Meredith grabbed him. Coming behind her, Jeff held up his pint of onion dip. Good old Jeff! He was right on schedule.

"Hey, look who's here!" Meredith said when she spotted Cathy. "Can you believe *live* music? At Smith's? We've been upgraded."

"Oh hi, Meredith. How come you're shopping so late?"

"Jeff forgot to buy dip for something at school, and *I* forgot this was the big singles' bash or I'd have come down by myself. I mean, what can you do with your son in tow, I ask you?"

Dale gritted his teeth. *Shut up, Meredith, shut up!*

"This is Singles' Night?" His mom gave the crowd a once-over. "Is that what the music's about?"

Meredith shrugged. "I guess. If I didn't know these two knuckleheads"—she hooked them around the neck—"I'd say they were in cahoots again."

Dale wrenched away. Jeff said "Us? Are you kidding? I've got homework stacked to the ceiling."

Dale's mother gave him a funny look before saying, "Get your chips, Dale. That's what we came for, remember?"

"Come with me," Dale said to Jeff, and they took off up Aisle Five, Dale making faces because of Meredith's big mouth. Maybe they should have told her, after all.

"There have been two people at the mike so far," Jeff hurried to fill in.

"How good were they?"

"He was gaggy, but she was—" His hand showed okay. "Anyhow, they got free tickets for Highway 101 just for being good sports. Don't you think we should tell your mom about the tickets before long?"

They could hear someone at the mike now, begging for more singers to step up and have a turn. Dale figured they weren't being swamped.

They found the chips, pivoted, and hurried back, which wasn't easy with the aisles so full. Mostly with women. There were a few guys and a couple of gray-haired grandpas having fun. There were also some teenagers who didn't belong there any more than they did.

Dale said, "Remember, you're the one who'll bring up the prize money. She'll get suspicious if I do. Mention the tickets if she acts stubborn. She loves concerts."

The group finally coaxed a cute single shopper into stepping up on the platform. She got some encouragement from the drummer, and people clapped. She went into a huddle with the musicians—checking their list of available songs, Dale guessed—and then they started in.

Unfortunately, she picked a Nanci Griffith number, "Love at the Five and Dime." Sung that lady's way, falling in love was something you'd want to avoid, whether it was at the Five and Dime, Smith's

Co-op, or the shoe repair. Dale could hardly keep from laughing. His mom was holding her sides, too, trying not to be rude.

Now's the time for reverse psychology, he thought suddenly, remembering how his mom used it on him.

"Wow, can she sing!" he gushed.

His mother shot him an unbelieving look and Meredith said, "Your son with the tin ear!" They cracked up.

The boys grinned at each other. So far so good. The moms were having a blast—Dale's singing along, Jeff's bouncing to the beat.

A minute later, Mrs. Jensen, a neighbor, crowded in to tell their moms about the prize money. Married as anything and embarrassed to be there, she'd just stopped by for breakfast rolls, she said, and saw the sign. "That's what it says out front. First prize, five hundred dollars. I'd go for it if I were you gals."

"Five hundred bucks!" Dale shouted. "Mom, you know you're better than that last one." *Forget psychology!*

"Sssshhhh!" she said, her face pink at the mention of all that money. "I'd look terrible in that hat they make you wear."

The hat! Was that all that was stopping her? A broad-brimmed white hat? Didn't his mom know gaucho was *in*? Paulette Carlson wore a Spanish-

169

style hat just like it on her album jacket.

"Big bucks!" the lead guitar was saying back at the mike. "Who's next? What about you cowboys? Here's a chance to live out that fantasy you've always had."

Meredith suddenly woke up. "Cathy, you idiot! Go on up there, you're a natural. Hey, you guys, ask *her*." She pointed to the top of Cathy's head, shouting, "Ask her!"

Too late. Someone else had already volunteered.

No competition, Dale decided, listening to someone else stumble through two verses she never knew in the first place.

It was the redheaded drummer's turn next, and that's when Dale began to suspect something was going on with his mom. During the entire drum solo—with this great rhythm engulfing them—she stood there next to him unmoving.

Taking deep breaths was what she was doing, enough to hyperventilate any normal person. When he saw her chin go up—like Lindsey's did when she was challenged—he knew what was coming.

"How about this lady in the red shirt?" one of the Gophers said after the drummer had finished.

"Go on, Mom, do it!" Dale whispered.

That's all it took. His mother struck out for the platform, her cheeks and eyes blazing like Matt's. The steel guitar slid through some happy chords and people let her through. Jeff whistled, Meredith looked scared. Dale just stood there, his heart drumming paradiddles on his ribs. The crowd waited, as if to see how bad this one would be.

The lead guitar player set the white hat straight across Dale's mom's head and adjusted it to fit her curls, the two of them talking the whole time. Dale figured she was asking for an intro to see if the key was right.

They gave her a few bars and she nodded.

Then she turned around, took the mike in her hand, smiled as if to say, "This, folks, is my very own territory!" and cut loose like Linda Ronstadt herself:

> *"I've been cheated, been mistreated,*
> *When will I be loved?*
> *I've been put down, I've been pushed 'round,*
> *When will I be loved?"*

Her voice drew shoppers out of the aisles like a magnet. She was great! He might be a tin-ear, but Dale knew *wonderful* when he heard it.

> *"When I find my new man that I want for mine*
> *He always breaks my heart in two*
> *It happens every time.*
>
> *"I've been made blue, I've been lied to,*
> *When will I be loved?"*

Soon the space around the platform was jammed. No one wanted her to quit after that first song, especially the guys in the band. The whole store clapped her back to the mike, including Mr. Ellis, who was suddenly standing there next to Meredith, smiling like it was all his idea.

The second go-around, she announced what she called "a little country number for the singles who shop at Smith's." She did "The Heart on My Sleeve" at full blast, swinging into the refrain with every woman there beating her hands together. And to think she'd been wasting her great voice singing over the vacuum cleaner!

Jeff kept poking him, but all Dale wanted was to shake his head or blink his eyes or something. His mom, Cathy Purcell, was a performer! He'd never heard her at a mike—didn't know she could sing like that. It was as if he were watching a stranger, someone else's mother who'd just happened in for oranges and got discovered.

Where was the lady he came with, the unhappy one who struggled with a big mortgage, three costly kids, and an old heap of a station wagon? The lady at the mike was *in charge*. She was full of smiles, a real crowd pleaser. His mother the singer was a sensation!

When she'd positively had enough, she told the lead guitarist she'd do one last song if she could dedicate it to the memory of her husband.

Dale sobered fast. He wasn't expecting that.

"But this is also for my son Dale," she said, "who—by very ingenious means—brought me down here to Smith's Co-op for such a fun time."

It was Dale's turn to melt—or die! Whichever came first.

When she called him up to the platform, he couldn't move. Waves of applause ricocheted off the steel beams, but he still couldn't get his feet going. It was little old Jeff who hauled him up in front of all those people to stand there and be hugged by his mom.

It probably wasn't possible, but Dale figured he held his breath all the way through her final number. "You're My Best Friend" would never sound so good to him again as it did right then.

chapter 17

Thursday, Dale and Jeff set up their "buffet" in a sunny place in the courtyard where Lizette and her two friends hung out during lunch period.

Once they'd spotted the girls, Jeff opened his carton of dip and put it between them on the stone bench. Dale tore open the chips and sampled one.

"Sure enough," he whispered, noticing the girls noticing them, "you don't have to advertise when you bite into one of these noisy potato chips."

All three girls came over, gushy and friendly as anything, saying "Give *us* some!" and "Is this, like, private, or can we crash?"

Lizette popped down on the bench next to Dale and helped herself. "You guys, I think we should get up a party for Okimoto's class. She's worked us to death the last nine months."

"My sentiments exactly," Jeff agreed.

Breakthrough! Three words—the first Jeff had spoken to Lizette all year.

"Ask Okimoto tomorrow," Megan said, nudging Dale with her shoe. "She likes you. I bet she'd let us if you ask."

Dale looked away. *I can't help it, Mom, all Okimoto wants to do is have parties.*

After a few more minutes, Jody, the restless one, said, "Come on, you guys, are we getting doughnuts or what?"

"Go ahead, I'll catch up." Lizette didn't move. She smiled at Dale instead. If his Ideal Girl got any closer, he'd need a paramedic.

All those practice conversations weren't helping him at all now that he was engaged in real talk. How come girls were so good at it? He couldn't think of a thing to say, just kept scooping up dip and shoving the stuff in his mouth. He wasn't even hungry.

"I heard about last night, and your mom," she said in voice that was low and confidential. "That's so neat."

"You should have been there." Jeff leaned over into their space, a regular talkathon host all of a sudden. "I mean, everybody thought she was great and they kept clapping her back for encores. I mean, she was awesome! Wasn't she, Dale?"

"I thought so." Dale swallowed a grin that was pure happiness now that he could feel Lizette's leg against his. "It's hard to be humble when you're a Purcell . . . but I'm working at it."

Lizette laughed. "What's she going to do with the five hundred dollars?"

"Pay the bills, she says. It'll be gone by the time I get home."

"Oh, how boring! Really, aren't you taking a trip or anything?"

"No, but Mom got a second job out of it. She's going to sing with the Gophers Friday and Saturday nights. I got a job out of it, too." He rolled his eyes like some medieval martyr. "I get to tend Matt."

"That's not fair," Lizette sympathized.

Dale shrugged. "She's paying me. And says she'll go half on a new mountain bike I've had my eye on at Guthrie's."

"Well"—Lizette stood up—"Mom says I'm too old for camp and too young for a job. Is that pitiful enough? I'm definitely going to be around this summer, so you guys call me if you get bored."

"Okay!" they said as one man.

"Wait—" She pulled out a pad of paper and wrote down her number. "It's unlisted. You'd never get it out of the operator." Tearing off the pink sheet, she handed it to Dale.

Pink! *Pink stationery.* He felt its weight, noted its size. He looked up. "You didn't . . . you weren't the one who stuck that note in my book, the one without any words?"

A slow smile took over her face. "A long time ago? Maybe. Why didn't you write back? I thought you very unfriendly, actually."

Dale felt his face getting hot. "But it didn't say anything," he blurted out, "not even your name."

She walked off with a wave of the fingertips. "Ever hear of disappearing ink? I thought you'd figure it out."

Dale and Jeff stared at each other, mouths open.

"Hey," Dale called after her, "is this phone number going to disappear?"

"Yes," she answered, laughing, "so you better memorize it."

So Lizette had kind of liked him way back then. Now Dale wasn't sure he could make it through the afternoon without a bypass.

Next to the great conversation with Lizette, the best thing that happened to Dale—to the whole family, really—was finding John at the door one night in May. It was close to dinnertime when the doorbell rang and Dale answered.

"Is your mother home?" John asked, after Dale greeted him with a big, surprised "Oh, hi!"

"She's here someplace. Come on in." Dale gave a quick look behind John to see if Kelli was along.

"She's at play practice," he explained. "Finally got a part after trying out all year. I guess persistence pays, huh?

"How have you been?" John asked, his clothes smelling like rain and the outdoors. He still had that great private-joke look on his face, as if he could hardly wait for whatever was coming next.

"Is Matt home yet?" he went on before Dale could answer.

"Nope. He's playing at Jamie's house, but he'll be here pretty soon. And Lindsey's still at the gym."

Just then his mom came out of the bathroom and started toward them along the hall.

"Oh!" She jumped seeing John. "I didn't know we had company. Dale, why didn't you call me?" She was embarrassed, he guessed, to be caught in her khaki workpants. Worse, she had her hair tied back and her face greased.

"Sorry," John apologized, "I should have called, but I was—"

"No, it's okay. Wait—let me tissue this off." She ducked back down the hall.

Dale motioned that John should sit down on the sofa or chair.

He didn't. He just stood there, looking around the living-room floor for something. Finally he said, "What happened to Century 21?"

Dale grinned. "Matt got well, that's what happened. We also built a Century 22 that day—on the linear plan—and a Century 23. Like the capital, with streets coming out. Gol, we had cities all over the place."

"A population explosion," John quipped, "in your own living room."

Dale's mom was in control when she showed up a minute later, wearing her clogs and asking John if he'd like some coffee. "I was just about to have a cup," she said, treating him to a smile. Dale knew she'd already finished the pot and put it in the sink.

When he accepted, they headed for the kitchen, with John still in his brown cord jacket. He had on work boots, so Dale figured he'd come straight from one of his inspection tours.

Dale hung back, listening to the coffee-making sounds and thinking they mightn't want him around. He was trying to decide if he should go over to Jeff's when he heard his mom say, "You did what? Oh no, you shouldn't have."

John's jolly laugh came rolling out of the kitchen next. "Well, I knew Matt had been sick a lot, and I thought a surprise might be good for him."

"I can't believe it!" she exclaimed, sounding as

excited as she had over the big bucks. "You are too nice! Dale, come in here."

He tore into the kitchen.

"John has a Brittany spaniel puppy out in his truck. For Matt." Her eyes misted up. "And get this! With a six-month supply of puppy food."

"Shots arranged for, too," he added. "I was taking a chance, not knowing if you really wanted a dog. But if you decide to keep him, I've also got a beginning dog owner's manual." He stood and pulled a paperback out of the rear pocket of his jeans. "Appropriately dog-eared," he said as he handed it to Dale. "It was Kelli's once, but she wants Matt to have it."

Dale couldn't stop smiling, imagining how excited Matt would be.

As soon as John left to bring in the puppy, his mother whipped off a paper towel and wiped the corners of her eyes. Dale turned his back and concentrated on paging through the book. His mom could get so emotional when people were nice to her. At least she wasn't still mad about what happened at Wendy's. Maybe now John and she could become friends.

It was only a few minutes before Matt walked in with the volume up, the way he always did, to find this brown-and-white spotted pup standing splay-legged in the middle of the floor. It was about one second before the dog was throwing himself at Matt—jumping, licking, whining, puppy-delighted to meet someone his own size.

Pulling the dog down on top of him, Matt crooned, "Waggy, Waggy! Nice boy! I knew you'd come someday."

No introductions needed. Matt knew exactly who it was licking his face, and was all but licking Waggy back.

Their mother wiped her eyes again, and Dale walked off to bury his head in the refrigerator. Too bad Lindsey wasn't there. Or their dad. What fun if everyone had been home to see Matt!

He poured a glass of milk, then busied himself finding an old margarine tub.

"Hey, Matt," he said a minute later, "bring him over and we'll see if he's hungry."

That's where they were when Lindsey got home—Dale, Matt, their mother, John—all down on the kitchen floor watching the two-month-old spaniel slop milk all over the kitchen floor.

"He's ours!" Matt yelled immediately. "We get to keep him. Forever!"

Lindsey dropped to the floor next to John. "Oh, how darling!" She reached out to feel the pup's silky head, the floppy ears, the big soft feet. Suddenly, *plop*! Down went Waggy on his back, wiggling every which way, a hind leg up and jerking. All hands were suddenly right there, patting and scratching the softest puppy belly ever.

It was their mom's idea to get Jeff and Meredith to drop everything and come right up to meet Waggy. Matt agreed, and Dale made the call. After all, it isn't every day you add a new member to the family.

A few minutes later, Jeff came bursting into the house. He didn't ring, knock, or anything. Meredith followed, with Christopher behind her. They'd been having a cramming session for finals, according to Jeff.

"How will I ever pass chemistry?" Meredith complained loudly. "Don't you know this is a serious interruption?"

Nobody cared. John stood up as Dale's mom introduced him, then they all crowded into the kitchen together. After a lot of excited talk and exclaiming, it seemed to dawn on Matt who this Christopher person was.

"Is that the undertaker?" he asked, his eyes easily as big as his mouth. Dale cringed. Why had he ever taught him that word?

Matt swung around to confront Dale, his look saying, "You invited *him*?"

"Matthew!" his mom scolded. "Christopher's a friend of ours. And the word we use nowadays is *mortician*."

Christopher threw up his hands and laughed. "It's okay, Matt, believe me. No one ever invites the undertaker. He just shows up." He squeezed Matt's neck as he dropped down to admire Waggy at close range. "What a beauty. I never saw such nice markings on a Brittany spaniel. I used to raise hunting dogs myself, you know."

Was there anything Christopher hadn't done? Dale wondered.

"You can pet him if you want to," Matt offered, hugging Waggy a little closer than was comfortable for a two-month-old, but offering nonetheless.

They all ended up going to Wendy's for dinner, with John insisting the treat be on him this time.

And Dale ended up doing what he said he never would.

When they couldn't all fit into the truck and his mom's car was blocked by the vehicles in the driveway, Christopher offered transportation. "Transportation" this time was a retired Caddie limo he'd picked up from Detweiler's at a price he couldn't resist. Once a shiny black, it was now spotted with reddish primer coat, but unmistakably the genuine article.

"Take my word," he assured them, opening all the doors, "there's plenty of room inside."

A little later, eight of them occupying three

Wendy's tables, end to end, Dale felt happiness inflating inside his chest like a balloon. Taken separately or together, their group tonight was the max! Meredith, John, his mom—all were single parents with kids; Christopher, who adopted whoever came along if they were willing to adopt him, was single without kids. There wasn't one traditional family at their table. He thought of yakky Carol in his English class and that day last fall when she'd made him feel somehow deficient for being in the twenty-four percent minority.

It's four out of four tonight, Carol, but we're all smiling. Well, all except Matt, maybe, who was sad because he'd temporarily had to leave Waggy at home in John's truck.

Dale's mom looked happier than anyone, telling about her winnings, about how Dale had enticed her down to Smith's and what happened. She'd since been to two rehearsals with the group, bought herself some genuine western boots, and was practicing at home with tapes. Even her "independent spiritual coordinator" (as Meredith was calling herself) had predicted smooth days ahead.

Later on, Dale heard his mom inviting John and Christopher to drop in at the Longhorn Inn where the Down Under Gophers appeared weekends. When they both promised they would, Dale and Jeff joyfully traded kicks under the table.

And all because of us, thought Dale, taking ample credit for how things were turning out.

"My mother the celebrity," he whispered across to Jeff, loud enough for everyone to hear and laugh.

How different tonight was from that other time at Wendy's. Dale had been so positive then that everything depended on him. He'd advertised and connived and all but given his mom away in an effort to keep their old life intact. Now, pumped up by all the good feelings, he was ready to face facts: a) Stuff happens to people; b) things change; and c) chances are, if you trust and help each other, you'll be happy again. The three steps were part of the last essay he wrote for English—"The ABC's of Survival"—one of a half dozen that ended up in the north hall display case.

The truth was, Dale was glad to hand the responsibility for the Purcell family back to his mom. He had his own plans and a million things to do. He might even keep a writer's journal starting in June. It was Mrs. Okimoto's idea, of course. She'd told him he had great potential if he wasn't too lazy to develop it. Good old Okimoto! Depend on her not to mince words.

Later that night, riding home in Christopher's formerly state-of-the-art limo with its dove-gray interior, the two boys slid down so far in the backseat that no one on the streets could possibly see them.

"So who's going to call her first?" Jeff asked at Dale's ear, as if the question had been smoldering for days.

"Call who?"

"Lizette, who else? Summer's almost here."

"We'll toss a coin," Dale said, awash with generosity.

Jeff dug in his pocket, came up with a dime. "Heads, I call her first."

"Suits me."

They traded a few elbow pokes, then Jeff got busy warming up his dime. He rubbed it between his palms, blew on it, whispered his private hopes into his hands.

Dale looked on and grinned. "Heads" would be okay with him. He'd been wanting to do something nice for Jeff for a long time now.

"Toss it," he said, feeling like a winner regardless of chance.